WITNESS PROTECTION BREACH

KAREN KIRST

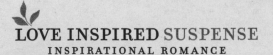

LOVE INSPIRED SUSPENSE

INSPIRATIONAL ROMANCE

LOVE INSPIRED® SUSPENSE
INSPIRATIONAL ROMANCE

Recycling programs for this product may not exist in your area.

ISBN-13: 978-1-335-58736-7

Witness Protection Breach

Love Inspired
22 Adelaide St. West, 41st Floor
Toronto, Ontario M5H 4E3, Canada
www.LoveInspired.com

Printed in U.S.A.

The flashlight beam glanced off her disheveled clothing and bloodied lip.

"What happened?"

"Someone grabbed me from behind and dragged me here." She brought her hand to her mouth and winced. Her moss green eyes were stark in her pinched face.

"You all right, Jade? Do you need a ride to the clinic?"

Her arms still wound tightly around her upper body, she shook her head. Pale threads of hair had escaped her braid. "I'm fine."

The sleeve of her black coat had been ripped free of the shoulder seam, evidence of the force of the man's grip.

Cruz worked hard to bottle his anger. He suspected what the perp's likely intent had been, and he was grateful Jade had been spared. She was a good person, a model citizen who'd probably never brushed shoulders with the criminal element. She shouldn't have to live with this haunting her for weeks, maybe months, to come. He would do everything in his power to run this guy to ground and make sure he didn't hurt anyone else.

Karen Kirst was born and raised in East Tennessee near the Great Smoky Mountains. She's a lifelong lover of books, but it wasn't until after college that she had the grand idea to write one herself. Now she divides her time between being a wife, homeschooling mom and romance writer. Her favorite pastimes are reading, visiting tearooms and watching romantic comedies.

Books by Karen Kirst

Love Inspired Suspense

Explosive Reunion
Intensive Care Crisis
Danger in the Deep
Forgotten Secrets

Smoky Mountain Defenders

Targeted for Revenge
Smoky Mountain Ambush
Mountain Murder Investigation
Witness Protection Breach

Visit the Author Profile page at LoveInspired.com for more titles.

But the God of all grace, who hath called us unto his eternal glory by Christ Jesus, after that ye have suffered a while, make you perfect, stablish, strengthen, settle you.
—*1 Peter* 5:10

To my mom, Dorothy Kirst.
I couldn't have asked for a better mom and friend.
I love you.

ONE

Somewhere in the square, a truck engine backfired, and Jade Harris choked on her steamed vanilla milk. The gunfire-like blast hauled her back in time to the seedy streets of Gainesville, Florida, and a life the US Marshals had erased in exchange for testimony against her drug-trafficker boyfriend. Jenny Hollowell—college cheerleader turned drug addict dropout—had been declared dead.

She wiped the whipped cream from her nose and resumed her stroll past the festive window displays that lit up the night. Serenity's town square had been transformed for the holidays, and residents and tourists alike had come out for the Victorian Christmas Extravaganza. What wasn't to like about twinkling lights, free treats in every shop, hayrides and carolers dressed like Charles Dickens's characters? She had about twenty minutes to finish her shopping before her five-year-old son, Henry, returned from the hayride with his part-time babysitter, Tessa Reed, and her daughter, Lily.

She crossed to the central, picturesque square. Wreaths hung on the lampposts. Lights sparkled like fireflies in bushes of various sizes and shapes, and tree trunks had been wrapped with bulbs that winked red and green. There were fewer people here, but those she passed smiled in greeting. Thanks to her job at Serenity's only vet clinic, she was a familiar face to many in town.

The brick path took her into an isolated, shadowed copse, and unease pinched her spine. She picked up the pace even as she scolded herself. The path curved, and she almost collided with a stranger. She yelped and jerked away. The man lifted his brows and, sidestepping, continued on his way.

There's nothing to fear here, remember?

Axel Ward was locked away in a Florida prison. What was more, he thought she was dead, taken out by the car bomb he'd had one of his associates plant.

The path curved again, and she emerged into an open area facing another line of shops. She stopped and inventoried her surroundings. Some people conversed outside the general store, enjoying the fudge and hot cider owner Bill was giving away. Others walked with purpose, shopping bags swinging from their arms. No one paid her any attention. In the distance, near the courthouse and library, she glimpsed a mounted police officer astride his horse. Could've been Mason Reed or Cruz Castillo. The shadows made it impossible to discern the horse's coloring.

Her irrational fears calmed by the sight, she entered the bookstore and found a book about trains for Henry. After making the purchase, she walked to the spare lot at the end of the complex to stow the gifts in the trunk before meeting up with Tessa and the kids.

Because she was envisioning Christmas morning and her little boy's reaction to her gifts, she didn't perceive the impending danger. By the time she heard the gravel dislodge and smelled the pungent odor of sweat and cigars, it was too late. There wasn't time to turn and confront whoever was behind her. A man's wide, callused hand smothered her mouth and nose. His other one clamped around her waist, one muscled arm lifting her off the ground and half propelling, half dragging her between the nearby trees.

Mounted Police Officer Cruz Castillo wasn't paying attention to the rumbling tractor near the courthouse or the families waiting for the next hayride around town. He had his eye on a group of rowdy teenagers whose playful shoving and taunts threatened to become a real brawl. He arched his back to relieve the stiffness brought on by a day in the saddle. His partner, Renegade, shifted his bulk and flicked his ears as if to say he, too, was ready for the event to end. The harness bells jangled as Cruz nudged the Tennessee Walker in the teenagers' direction. Sometimes all it took to ward off trouble was the arrival of a thousand-pound horse in official police gear.

The boys noticed their approach, and the roughhousing began to subside. Cruz's attention shifted to a pint-size figure off to their left, and his gaze narrowed. A towheaded boy darted in between the cluster of people, his elfin face twisted in worry as he stopped and turned first one way and then another.

Henry Harris, the only child of his closest neighbor, Jade.

Although much of Cruz's police work was accomplished from the saddle, he dismounted and guided Renegade to the boy.

"Hey, buddy." Cruz crouched down and touched his shoulder.

"I can't find my mommy, Mr. Cruz."

Jade must be out of her mind with worry. She was devoted to Henry, attentive and nurturing while being firm in discipline. In that aspect, she reminded Cruz of his own mother.

Beneath the mop of tousled blond hair, Henry's big green eyes were shiny, a sure sign waterworks were inevitable if Cruz didn't act fast.

"I'll help you search. Wanna ride with me?"

The boy sniffled and tilted his head to get a good look at Renegade. "Is he nice like Gunsmoke and Old Bob?"

Henry had ridden Cruz's personal horses on several occasions. His pasture abutted Jade's rental property, and, shortly after they'd moved in, Henry had sneaked in to get a closer look at the horses. Cruz had been inspecting the paddock gate and had spotted him. He'd introduced him to the horses and given him a ride.

"Renegade's sweeter than baby's breath." Cruz lifted the boy onto his partner's back and climbed on behind him. He took the reins in hand and curled his arm around Henry's middle. "Did your mom go for a snack? Or to the bathroom?"

He shook his head vehemently. "She's shopping."

Henry's fingers clamped onto Cruz's wrist, and he was struck by his size and vulnerability. Good thing they'd crossed paths. The event was packed. A long-standing tradition, the Victorian Christmas Extravaganza drew people from surrounding towns, as well as tourists visiting the Smoky Mountains for the holidays.

Cruz searched the crowd for the petite vet tech, whose long snow-blond locks, pale skin and vivid green eyes made her stand out. "Do you remember what color coat she's wearing?"

Henry thought about it. "Uh-uh."

"That's all right." Cruz signaled Renegade forward. They hadn't gone far when he heard his name being called. He turned his head and saw his sergeant's wife, Tessa, hurrying toward them with their four-year-old daughter, Lily, in tow. Her stricken expression crumpled when she spotted the boy.

"Henry!" Her breath came out in a whoosh. "I've been looking everywhere for you!"

"I have to find my mommy."

Beneath the halo of black curls, Tessa's hazel eyes were troubled when she looked at Cruz. "I took the kids on a hayride. There were a lot of people waiting to take the next ride, and I lost track of Henry. I thought maybe he'd gone to the courthouse steps to meet Jade. She's not there. I've texted and called her several times."

He patted Henry's middle. "Change of plans, buddy. I want you to go with Tessa and Lily."

He stiffened. Tessa must've noticed the brewing protest, because she placed a hand on Henry's leg. "Let's go get those gingerbread cookies we talked about. We'll pick one out for your mom, too."

The starch went out of him, and Cruz lowered the boy into Tessa's waiting arms.

"Text me her contact information, will you?"

Tessa fished her phone from her coat pocket. His phone chimed, and he attempted to reach Jade as he and Renegade passed a group of carolers and entered the square. He used his police radio to alert his sergeant, Mason, and the other unit officers of his plans. While there was no reason to suspect trouble, his partners agreed to join in the search. Raven Ferrer was near the Black Bear Café and would have a look around as soon as she handed off an inebriated customer to a patrol officer. Silver Williams and Mason would start at opposite ends of the square and work their way along the shops.

From his vantage point, he could see Mason near the Mint Julep Boutique, but the trees in the center blocked his view of the daycare and the shops on the other side. He continued on, looking through the store windows for a glimpse of Jade. Had she decided to duck into Spike's for a burger? Or gotten caught up in conversation with someone?

He observed a pair of adult males conversing outside the restrooms, which capped the end of this row. He would ask if they'd seen Jade and, failing that, knock on the women's restroom door. Next on his list was the temporary parking area roped off behind the shops.

A shout broke into his thoughts, and Renegade was leaping into action almost before he gave the cue. The men raced into the trees. He couldn't make out their words, but he sensed their urgency. He activated his heavy-duty flashlight and navigated to the other side. The chaotic scene he encountered in the thickest part of the copse hardened his gut and released a flood of adrenaline through his system.

There was no denying the woman the two men were helping off the ground was Jade. Her hair gleamed like an iridescent pearl against black sand. The flashlight beam glanced off her disheveled clothing and bloodied lip. Heat flushed through his veins, and his muscles quivered with the need to avenge her. Violence against women and children never failed to trip his temper. He scoured the area for a target to zero in on.

After relaying his status over the radio, Cruz nudged Renegade closer.

"What happened, Jade?"

"Someone grabbed me from behind and dragged me here." She brought her hand to her mouth and winced. Her moss-green eyes were stark in her pinched face.

"Officer, we heard the scuffle and came running." The taller of the two men spoke up. He pointed in the direction of the main road. "The guy took off that way."

"Did he speak to you? Communicate his intent?" Cruz asked Jade.

"No." She wrapped her arms around herself, and he noticed her knuckles were cut up.

Mason arrived on his horse, Scout, and radioed the suspect's possible escape route to the others. The patrol officers would take charge of the search.

"You all right, Jade?" Mason inquired, his brown eyes somber. "Do you need a ride to the clinic?"

Her arms still wound tightly around her upper body, she shook her head. Pale threads of hair had escaped her braid. "I'm fine."

The sleeve of her black coat had been ripped free of the shoulder seam, evidence of the force of her attacker's grip.

"I'll take these gentlemen's statements." Mason gestured to Jade. "Cruz?"

They'd worked together long enough to develop a sort of nonverbal shorthand. He understood his sergeant's wishes without being told.

Cruz dismounted and approached Jade. She dropped her arms and took a step back, lips parted, eyes wide. He stopped, surprised by the reaction. He wasn't a stranger. He certainly wouldn't ever hurt her.

He took his time scooping up her discarded packages and held out his other hand.

"Walk with me?"

She glanced at the spot on the ground where she'd been attacked, and a shudder racked her body. Ignoring his hand, she started walking. "I need to get to Henry."

Cruz took Renegade's lead rope and used the flashlight to illuminate their path. "Henry was worried. I found him searching for you. He slipped away from Tessa."

"What?" Her stride lengthened. "Where is he now?"

"With Tessa and Lily."

She would've burst into a jog if he hadn't lifted his arm as a barrier. "Hold up a second. I know you're eager to see him, but I have to get your full statement. More importantly, we need to address your wounds."

"But—"

"You don't want him to see you like this, Jade." He lightly touched the rip in her coat sleeve, and she jumped. "We'll get those scrapes bandaged, okay?"

Her fingers worried the silver cross dangling from a thin chain at her neck. "Okay."

Cruz worked hard to bottle his anger. He suspected what the perp's likely intent had been, and he was grateful Jade had been spared. He would do everything in his power to run this guy to ground and make sure he didn't hurt anyone else.

TWO

Jade couldn't stop trembling. This wasn't the first or even the second time she'd been roughed up, but it had been years since she'd escaped Gainesville's criminal underbelly. She'd gotten used to people treating her with kindness and respect. She'd gotten soft. The attack had rattled her to the core, a harsh reminder that violence exacted a mental toll. She felt as if the stranger's hands were still on her, his breath on her neck, his malicious intentions infusing her with dread.

The hair that escaped her French braid dangled limply around her face. Her attempts to weave the strands into place failed, so she removed the elastic band and used her fingers to comb out the tangles.

Cruz crouched beside the folding table closest to the police tent's entrance and riffled through a duffel bag. It was impossible not to notice the ripple of taut muscles beneath his blue-black uniform shirt. Her gaze moved upward to the tanned, smooth skin above his starched collar. He'd removed his helmet, and his short black hair was damp at the temples, the longer top strands in disarray. He retrieved a navy blue Serenity Mounted Police sweatshirt and brought it to her.

When they'd entered the white canvas tent, he'd set a

metal chair next to the snack table for her. Now he placed a second chair facing her, lowered his body onto it and slid the first aid kit closer to himself.

She murmured her thanks and, after shucking her torn coat, pulled the sweatshirt over her head. His cologne clung to the material—a sultry, musky scent perfect for a heart-stopping cowboy type. But she couldn't separate his Texas roots from his current career. Police in general made her antsy, even though she was no longer on the wrong side of the law.

Cruz Castillo's profession wasn't the only reason he got under her skin. Over six feet tall with a strapping build, he was the kind of man you didn't dismiss or forget, whether in uniform or in his usual shirt, jeans and cowboy boots. His jet-black hair and short goatee enhanced his wide fore-head, defined cheekbones and angular jaw. His cocoa-colored eyes were sharp with intelligence and seemed to cut through lies like a laser.

Twisting the lid off a water bottle, he reached for her hand. She sucked in a breath when his warm, callused fingers wrapped around her palm. A pleasant sensation tickled her skin. The contact was nice.

His eyes flashed an apology. "I'll be as gentle as I can."

Holding her hand above the grass, he poured water over the busted knuckles and pressed a clean cloth to them. She stared at his bent head, at the hint of wave in his thick locks. This was the closest she'd ever been to him.

"I fought to get away from him," she blurted, thrown off-kilter by her reaction.

He lifted his head. "Good thinking. You delayed him long enough for those men to intervene."

Framed by his beard, his lips were full and beautiful. Mortified and confused by the thought, she pressed her own together and experienced a shimmer of pain.

His forehead creased. "I'll get you a wet cloth for that lip."

"How bad does it look? Will Henry notice?"

"Henry's as bright as a new penny. You may want to prepare a tactful answer in case he does."

He was still holding her hand carefully. She'd seen his gentleness with her son on multiple occasions. She hadn't experienced it for herself, however. Thankfully, he made quick work of doctoring her wounds with antibiotic cream and bandages.

"I need you to walk me through what happened." He took a small notebook from his uniform pocket and held his pen aloft.

He looked somber but also riled. He was angry on her behalf. Imagine that, from a cop.

Cruz's polite manner would disappear if he learned of her sordid past. His loathing for drugs was no secret. He'd made it his personal mission to drive them out of Serenity and to convince students not to succumb to peer pressure or curiosity. He wouldn't learn her secret, though. The locals thought she'd led a run-of-the-mill, standard American life, which was the truth—up until she'd struck up a fateful friendship with the wrong man.

Jade ran her palms over her pants and, noticing a slight tear, began to pick at it.

"I went into several shops and purchased gifts for Henry. I headed to my car to put them in the trunk before meeting up with Tessa and the kids. As I was passing the restroom, hc grabbed me from behind and dragged me into the trees."

"Did your attacker say anything?"

"No."

His silence had unnerved her. It was as if she was less than human and didn't deserve to be spoken to.

"Did you get a look at his face? Notice any features?"

"He was behind me the whole time. I struggled and got free, but I tripped and fell. As I was trying to get up, he struck me." She touched her busted lip. "I crawled away. He seized the back of my neck. The next thing I know, the men were shouting and running, and he fled."

A muscle in his cheek twitched. "Are there any details you can give me? Height? Build?"

Jade closed her eyes. "He was quite a bit taller than me."

"You're, what? Somewhere around five-four?"

She nodded and continued with her description of her attacker. "His muscles were exaggerated, like he spends a substantial amount of time in the gym."

His hand had seemed powerful enough to snap her neck like a toothpick.

"Do you recall any specific smells?"

"Cigar. Sweat."

"He didn't try to take your purse, phone or jewelry?"

"No." Fear jolted her as her mind landed on what he might've wanted with her. She quickly stood. "That's all I remember. Can I go to Henry now?"

Cruz got to his feet as well, and tucked his notebook in his pocket. He towered over her, and she had to tilt her head to meet his gaze.

"Did you notice anyone suspicious around you tonight?"

"Everyone I encountered was in happy spirits."

He hooked his thumb over his shoulder. "I'll walk with you."

She didn't try to talk him out of it. The big Texan's presence was exactly what she needed right now.

"I'll compare my notes with Mason's. But I want you to be prepared in the event we don't locate this guy. We have very little to go on."

She swallowed her nervousness and gathered her shopping bags. "I understand."

"This is what I'd call an attack of opportunity. You were alone. The noise and activity made him bold. I don't foresee you having this kind of trouble again." His brows crashed together. "I am sorry this happened to you."

He swept open the tent flap and greeted Renegade. "You remember Jade, don't you? She's the one who gives you extra treats after your shots."

"You noticed?" She ran her hand along the horse's neck, wishing she could hug him until the ordeal faded from memory.

He untied the lead rope. "I'm trained to notice important details. Renegade is your favorite, isn't he?"

"I can't confirm nor deny."

"Don't worry, your secret is safe with me."

She shifted her gaze to her tennis shoes. If he only knew her entire life was a secret. Sometimes, she felt the urge to tell someone. She felt so alone in this giant, extravagant lie. Her one consolation? It was keeping her and Henry safe.

Cruz accompanied her to the bakery and waited with Renegade right outside. Henry's face lit up when he saw her. "Mommy!"

He launched himself forward, and Jade crouched to catch him, almost tipping over backward in the process. His hug was fierce. He smelled sweet and gingery, like the cookie crumbles around his mouth. She held his slight body close, tears welling up.

What if he'd gotten lost looking for her? What if the stranger had gotten her into a vehicle?

Thank You, Jesus, for watching over me and my boy.

He broke the hug, his adoration shifting to accusation in a blink of an eye, five-year-old style. "Where were you?"

She tenderly brushed the scruffy bangs off his forehead. "I got delayed." Trying to distract him, she motioned to the table he shared with Tessa and Lily. "Did you save me a cookie?"

Lily called his name and urged him to go look at something in the bakery case with her. Quick as a blink, he forgot their conversation and left with his friend.

Tessa leaned forward, her eyes apologetic. "Jade, I feel terrible. He melted into the crowd while I was helping Lily off the tractor. I called his name, but he was already gone. I guess searching for you. I'm sick over it, truly."

Jade put a hand on her friend's arm. "It could've happened to anyone. In fact, he's done it to me at the park a time or two. I'll have a talk with him tomorrow."

Tessa noticed her bandaged hand, and her frown intensified. "Where's your coat? And why is Cruz guarding the door?"

"Not here." There were too many people around who could overhear. "Let's get the kids into the truck first."

It wasn't easy to pull the kids away from the colorful array of desserts, but they gathered up their cookies and finished them off as they exited.

After greeting Tessa, Cruz put on his helmet and adjusted the strap. Inserting one boot into the stirrup, he effortlessly seated himself in the saddle.

She and Tessa walked directly behind the kids, with Cruz bringing up the rear. Jade felt better once Henry was buckled into his booster seat and Lily was bouncing on the seat beside him. Cruz stationed himself at the hood of the truck, affording her and Tessa a modicum of privacy. When she'd relayed the news, Tessa hugged her with a fierce protectiveness that again had Jade fighting emotion.

Lord, thank You for second chances, for blessing me with this new life and friends who love and support me.

"Do you want to stay at our house tonight?"

"Don't tempt me." She shook her head. "We'll be fine."

"Call if you change your mind. Or if you can't sleep and need someone to talk to."

"I will."

"I mean it, no matter what time."

"All right."

Tessa and Lily bade Cruz good-night and went in search of Mason.

Jade lightly gripped the truck's door handle. "Thank you, Cruz, for everything."

He inclined his head. "You'll see my number on your phone. Store it. And remember, if you need me, I'm right next door."

She averted her face, hiding her surprise. Although they'd been neighbors for a long time, he'd kept his distance. They certainly didn't swap cups of sugar and juicy bits of news across the fence.

Jade told him good-night, and he signaled Renegade to back up. She felt the weight of his stare as she got behind the wheel, started the engine and eased out of the space. During the ride home, Henry chattered about the hayride. Jade made adequate noises in response, but her mind whirled with tonight's events, touching repeatedly on Cruz Castillo.

His opinion of her was a mystery. Although their social and professional lives overlapped, he hadn't initiated a friendship with her. He was clearly uninterested in getting to know her better. Was it because she was a single mom? He stuck with his fellow officers and close buddies, often hanging out at the Black Bear Café listening to live bands and playing cornhole on the patio. He wasn't known to date locals…and not due to lack of opportunities. She'd seen women flirting with him. Overheard them ask him out. She'd also heard him politely decline.

Tessa had let it slip that he'd left an ex-wife behind in Texas, but she hadn't shared details. Apparently, Cruz was closemouthed about his past. Jade could commiserate.

Thoughts of the enigmatic Texan scattered as the white Craftsman house they called home came into view. The single front porch light no longer seemed adequate. Parking beneath the live oak tree that hugged the paved drive, she studied the darkened side windows. As her anxiety ramped up, she gave herself a stern scolding. She'd been on her own for years, and she'd managed to keep herself and her son safe. Cruz was right. The attack was a random, isolated event. This night, she told herself firmly, would soon be nothing more than an uncomfortable memory.

Still, she rushed Henry inside, flipping on lights and testing the doors and windows. While he splashed and played in the bath, Jade stepped into the hallway and connected with her friend Leslie via video chat.

Leslie Harding was the first friend she'd made after entering the protection program. Jade had been relocated to Knoxville and had gotten a job at a convenience store as a means to support herself while pursuing her degree. The older and wiser Leslie had seen the lonely, bruised heart behind her bravado and befriended her. She'd showered her with love and compassion. She'd taken her to church. And when Jade had learned of her pregnancy and become overwhelmed, Leslie had prayed with her, encouraged her, supported her. Most importantly, she'd introduced her to her Savior, Jesus Christ.

"Jade." Leslie's brown eyes sparkled behind her paisley-print glasses. Her vivid red blouse was the perfect foil for her luminescent black skin and hair. The room around her buzzed with music and laughter.

Jade had forgotten tonight was her friend's annual Christmas party and apologized for interrupting.

"I'm happy to hear from you," Leslie told her. "How was the extravaganza?"

Jade rushed out an explanation in a wobbly voice. Immediately, Leslie's features shifted into motherly concern. "I'll come over."

"I don't want you to leave your party." Leslie and her husband had two grown sons and a wide circle of friends. It was an hour's drive from her home in Knoxville to Serenity. "I just wanted you to know. To pray."

Leaning against the wall across from the open bathroom door, she peeked at Henry. Coated in bubbles, he held action figures in each hand and was carrying on a conversation with an imaginary companion.

"You have my prayers, of course. But you can have me there, too. Gerard can handle hosting duties."

"I'm fine, Leslie. Just rattled."

"You're sure?"

"Positive." Her attacker didn't know her name or where she lived.

They made plans to meet the following weekend and ended the call.

Jade got Henry into pajamas and under his covers. Thanks to the day's excitement, he wasn't ready for sleep. She turned off the overhead fixture, and the bedside lamp bathed the room in soothing light. She got comfortable beside him, the padded headboard supporting her back, and retrieved the stack of books from the bedside table. They just might make it through all of them tonight before he dozed off.

Jade was halfway through the second book when she heard the telltale creak. The top step of her back deck was warped and always made a distinctive noise. Her heartbeat kicked into overdrive.

"What is it, Mommy?"

Schooling her features, she handed him the book. "I'll be right back."

Gripping her phone in her palm, she tiptoed through the living room and into the kitchen. The wicker light fixture above the round white table and chairs cast odd patterns through the room. Ahead, flanked by a storage closet and laundry room, the back door was shut and the lock engaged. The door seemed solid enough, but for the first time she was aware of the glass insert. Suddenly, she was viewing her home through a security lens. Working up her courage, she walked to the door, flipped on the porch light and drew the curtain aside.

The deck furniture hadn't been disturbed. The stairs were empty.

False alarm.

She let out the breath she'd been holding in one short burst. As she started to turn away, she saw someone standing between the trees and fence that marked Cruz's property line. Someone was out there.

Her phone slipped from her fingers and clattered to the floor.

THREE

"I'm sorry, Jade. I didn't mean to frighten you." Cruz closed and locked the back door, shutting out the biting cold. She'd called him in a panic, not realizing he was the one who'd spooked her. "Gunsmoke wandered down this way and wouldn't respond to my calls. He can be stubborn sometimes."

Jade was stationed in the galley kitchen near the stainless steel stove, both hands worrying the cross pendant at her throat. A gold ring adorned her right ring finger, and the jade stone glinted in the overhead light. She still wore his sweatshirt. The casual garment didn't mesh with her usual elegant style. Even when on vet duty, she wore crisp collared shirts with floral or geometric prints and dainty buttons. Her nails were always painted, her jewelry minimal and her hair held back either in a braid or with a barrette. Now her hair cascaded around her shoulders like a drift of freshly fallen snow, and his heart kicked like a wily stallion each time he looked her in the eye. Not a pleasant state of affairs.

Walking around the table, he stopped and leaned against the farmhouse sink. "I should've called and let you know I'd be out there."

She ran her tongue over her busted lip. "I thought I heard someone on the deck and overreacted."

He hated that someone had shattered her peace and that he'd compounded the problem. He didn't know her well enough to guess how long this would affect her.

The patter of feet in the living room behind her heralded Henry's arrival. "Mr. Cruz, will you read me a story?"

Henry's hair was damp and combed off his face. The traces of dirt, sweat and treats had been wiped away, and he stood there, fresh and clean in striped cotton pajamas. The boy had his mother's moss-green eyes, pale hair and rounded chin. Did he resemble his father at all? Cruz's curiosity flared to life, and he suddenly had a burning desire to know more about Jade's pre-Serenity life.

"Will you?"

Jade didn't offer any objections, and Cruz couldn't deny him. "Sure. What's it about?"

"A Christmas donkey." Henry snagged Cruz's hand and tugged.

"A donkey, huh?"

Their two-bedroom bungalow had the living room and second bedroom at the front of the house. Henry's bedroom was a spectrum of blue, from powder to navy, with white walls and white furniture. His lamp was shaped like a star. There were toy bins, a dresser and a rug made to look like a racetrack. Jade had certainly infused the older house with charm and warmth.

Henry snuggled under the covers and patted the mattress. Following the boy's lead, Cruz removed his boots and found a spot on the bed. He noticed Jade hovering in the doorway, observing, and felt a nervous quiver in his belly. Jade wasn't out to snag a husband. She hadn't ever given off that vibe. Why, then, did he wish she wouldn't listen to him read?

Henry leaned against him, and he automatically curved his arm around the boy. An odd ache gripped him. If he and Denise had found a way to make their marriage work, would he have a son of his own by now?

Licking his dry lips, he turned the page and mustered on. When he'd finished that one, Henry scrambled for another.

Jade held up her finger. "You said one, Henry." Her pale pink lips curved slightly in Cruz's direction. "Around here, one can easily become a dozen."

"You don't mind, do you?" Henry entreated.

"I don't mind, but Gunsmoke and Old Bob probably do. They're waiting on me to put them to bed."

"Will you read to me tomorrow night?"

Jade blushed to the roots of her hair.

Cruz chuckled and ruffled the boy's pale locks. "Good night, Henry."

She admonished Henry to remain in bed this time and, pulling the door almost closed, trailed Cruz into the living room. The furniture was mismatched and well loved. There were candles and books set about and a geometric-pattern rug on the oak floors. A white artificial tree was tucked between the couch and an armchair, and it was decorated like a package of gumdrops in tones of pink, green and blue.

He wandered to a collection of picture frames on a side table. "Who's this?"

"My dear friends, Leslie and Gerard Harding. You may have seen them around. They visit us from time to time. They like the Black Bear almost as much as you do."

"Too much of my paycheck goes to that place, but it seems pointless to cook for one." He liked to use his smoker and grill, but he didn't have the patience for any sides other than rice. He was sure his mother didn't count the green peppers and onions in his *arroz verde*. She would say he needed more vegetables in his diet…if she wasn't too busy interrogating him about his love life. "Where did you live before Serenity?"

"Knoxville."

"That's your hometown?"

"No. Florida."

"Where in Florida?"

Her smile seemed practiced, and his internal alarm ticked a warning.

"An insignificant town on the Gulf Coast. You wouldn't know it."

Her evasiveness bothered him. "No photos of your folks?"

"We're not on good terms." She twisted the jade ring round and round. "Leslie and Gerard are my family now."

Her firm tone cautioned against more questions. When she covered a yawn, he moved to the door. "You've got church in the morning. I'll get going."

She leaned her hip into the couch and cocked her head, her hair spilling over one shoulder. "I haven't seen you there in a while."

Distracted by the play of light in her lustrous hair, he said, "I figured going because it's expected wasn't benefiting anyone."

Questions flitted over her face that he chose to answer—in part.

"My relationship with God isn't what it used to be."

His mom and grandmother were heartbroken over it. Bothered his father, too, but he didn't ask Cruz weekly if he was going to church.

"I'm sorry to hear that. I put my trust in Him in the early days of my pregnancy, and I've never once regretted it. He's everything to me."

The peace and confidence wrapped up in her words were alluring, and, for a moment, Cruz yearned for the closeness he'd once experienced with God. But then he remembered how God had allowed his nineteen-year-old brother to be gunned down by drug runners, how God had allowed his wife to walk away, to give up on their marriage. Bitterness, anger and regret were rooted deep inside him, and he couldn't see past them to the hope and optimism he used to have.

"Good night, Jade."

Striding to his truck, he scanned the darkened yard, the road and the Lambert farm across the way. If he was still a praying man, he'd ask the Lord to keep Jade and little Henry safe. But praying hadn't helped Sal. Hadn't helped his marriage. God wasn't listening to him anymore.

Jade parked her truck outside the farmers' co-op the next day. Brief bursts of wintry air rustled the bushes hugging the bright red buildings laid out in a linear fashion. Overhead, woolen clouds stretched across the sky. She'd allowed Henry to go home with Lily after the morning service and would soon be joining him there for the mounted police unit's Christmas party. Mason and Tessa had become dear friends, and she was happy they treated her and Henry as part of their extended family. The other officers didn't seem to mind when she horned in on unit functions. Mason's mom, Gina, and sister, Candace, were frequently in attendance, as well. The group was expanding in other ways, with both Silver and Raven having gotten married this year. She wondered how Cruz felt about being the last single one in the group, but she wasn't going to pose that question to him. He'd think she was asking because of a romantic reason and give her an even wider berth.

His expression as he'd walked out her door last night

was imprinted on her brain. What had driven a wedge between him and God? She knew very little about his family, only that he'd lost his older brother as a teen to drugs. Her heart grew heavy at the thought. She'd seen too many people die during her time with Axel—either to overdoses or to the violence of associating with drug pushers. She'd been too wrapped up in her own addictions to care that much then. Now that she was living a clean, redeemed life, she grieved the unnecessary losses.

If Cruz knew about her past, would he have even answered her call last night?

Through her windshield, she watched an old Oldsmobile cruise slowly past on the two-lane road. The car had pulled out behind her at the Mountain Side Inn, but she hadn't given it any thought. Her hand clenched around her phone, fingers poised to call for help. But the car continued down the road, and she relaxed. She hoped this hyperalertness would fade soon.

Looping her purse strap over her shoulder, she walked inside the co-op at a purposefully slow pace. She wasn't in danger. There was no need to act like she was.

Gary, the part-time clerk, was half draped over the register, staring at his phone. He offered a limp wave. She was the only customer in this main section, which housed home goods, apparel and pet supplies. Sunday afternoons were slow, even during the holiday season. Taking a cart, she left the building and traversed the covered walkway bordered by small-engine tractors. She entered the warehouse portion, bypassing industrial feed and fertilizer. The fresh wreaths and garlands her boss wanted for the clinic were stored in the deep recesses of the warehouse. The cart wheels bumped along the cement floor as she traversed the wide aisles between tall metal shelves.

Jade located the greenery and began stacking wreaths

in the cart. Her body was sore in odd places, a reminder of last night's tussle with a stranger. As she was reaching for the last wreath, she was bumped from behind. Before she could turn around or speak, something hard looped around her throat and cut off her air supply.

Panicked, she clawed at the unyielding object. The attacker's hot breath wafted over her cheek, and she shuddered.

She stomped on his foot, but he only grunted. He tugged her against him and pinned her arms to her sides, never letting up on the garrote.

Air. She needed air.

Her lungs strained. Her heart thundered.

She kicked her heel up and back, catching him in the inner thigh. He growled and cinched the object tighter around her throat. Her skin burned. Her head felt lighter than her body.

Gray static danced in her peripheral vision.

Before she lost consciousness, she asked God to watch over her son.

FOUR

The smell of pungent earth invaded Jade's nostrils. She lay on something soft and damp, and her body was being gently rocked. Her eyelids were heavy and unresponsive at first. When she finally coaxed them open, her surroundings didn't make sense. Metal coated with orange rust surrounded her. Above, there was nothing but gray sky. Frosty air washed over her skin. Her fingers curled into the foreign material beneath her and came away trailing bits of mulch. The grunt and strain of a truck engine registered, and everything came at her at once.

She'd been abducted from the co-op. This wasn't a random crime of opportunity. Someone had an agenda, and she was the target.

Terror pushed her into action. Where was she? Where was he taking her? She crawled on her hands and knees to the back of the dump truck. The driver downshifted, knocking her forward, and she smacked her forehead on the metal gate. Blood trickled down her nose. Grasping the top edge, she gained her footing and peered over at rolling fields and a barn. Jade recognized the country road. In a few miles, the sporadic farms would give way to uninhabited land and a garbage dump. She wasn't about to stick around and find out what her abductor had in mind for her.

She had to escape, for Henry's sake.

The dump truck wasn't able to travel at a high rate of speed here—a point in her favor. She studied the pavement shunting past and gauged the risks. A broken bone was the least of her worries. It took her several tries to hook her knee over the top ledge and climb over. Her grip wasn't as sure as she'd thought, and she fell to the ground before she was ready. The impact jarred the breath from her lungs and wrenched her shoulder. The momentum rolled her into the ditch, among discarded trash and a child's sneaker.

Jade lay in the weeds, panting, taking stock of her injuries and praising God she'd made it out. She checked her coat pockets before remembering her phone was in her purse. Had she dropped that at the co-op? The truck's brakes squealed, and her relief disappeared like a vapor. Had he seen her escape?

She got up and ran. Ran until her head pounded, her lungs screamed for mercy and her injured shoulder couldn't endure another jarring step. Bent at the waist, her hands braced against her knees, she gulped mouthfuls of air that felt like ice shards in her throat. Sweat mixed with the blood from her head wound and dripped down her face.

A car approached, and she waved both arms. The teenage girl behind the wheel slammed on the brakes and stared, jaw hanging low. Jade rapped on the passenger window. The girl rolled it down an inch.

"Please, I'm in trouble. Can you take me to the police station?"

Her head bobbed, and Jade didn't hesitate. Buckling her seat belt, she introduced herself while peering through the foggy windshield. If her abductor had noticed her escape, he would've had to find a suitable place to turn the cumbersome vehicle around.

"I'm Sarah." The girl hung on to the wheel, wide eyes taking in Jade's appearance.

"I appreciate your help, Sarah."

With a nod, she removed her foot from the brake and did a U-turn in the middle of the road. Sarah let her borrow her cell phone, and Jade called the Serenity Police Station and explained the situation so they could send an officer in search of the dump truck. She also reached out to her WITSEC handler, Alan Prescott, and got his voice mail. That wasn't unusual. Although a busy man, he typically returned her calls within forty-eight hours. With Sarah in the car, Jade couldn't leave a detailed message, so she simply asked him to call her. Prescott would've already been in contact if there'd been a change in her case, of course, but she couldn't help worrying.

Axel Ward was a notorious drug trafficker whose influence and reach wouldn't be diminished by his incarceration. Back in Gainesville, the mere mention of his name was enough to incite fear. He not only pushed product that resulted in people's deaths, he ordered the murders of rivals, officials and anyone else who dared cross him. If he ever found out she was alive, he'd come after her. That was why she was very careful to follow the US Marshals' instructions.

At the station, she was met in the parking lot by Officer James Bell. He accompanied her inside and pointed her to a corner office. She sank gratefully into the cushioned chair across from his desk and accepted the paper cup he offered. Didn't matter that she hadn't had a drop of coffee—or any caffeinated beverage—in years. The rich, hot brew soothed her parched throat.

"Tell me what happened," he said gently. "Try to include all the details. Nothing is too small or insignificant."

Holding the cup between her palms, she replayed the

events in her mind and got the words out in stilted bursts. James's head was bent over his desk while he copied them down. She wished it was Cruz taking her statement, but he worked out of the mounted police stables.

The station door opened, and the man himself ambled through it. His fleece-lined black canvas coat was open to reveal a plaid button-down shirt. The top buttons weren't fastened, revealing a startling white T-shirt underneath. He spoke to the receptionist, who must've pointed him in her direction. When he turned his head, his chocolate gaze widened. His leather boots pounded on the chipped tile floor. After a swift inventory of her person, he barked James Bell's name.

James's pen clinked onto the desk and rolled off. At the reprimand in Cruz's voice, the dark-haired man looked at Jade with fresh eyes and flushed. "Sorry, Ms. Harris. I didn't think." Palms on the desk, he pushed back his chair. "The first aid kit's in the break room—"

"I'll handle it. Come with me, Jade."

She set the cup down and stood, unsure where this rush of warm feelings was coming from. His hand settled on her lower back as he guided her down the hall, deeper into the one-story building. His closeness was reassuring, but the blended scents of leather and musky cologne clinging to his clothes and skin sent her pulse reeling again.

"How did you know I was here?"

"Bell contacted Mason."

"Why would he do that?"

"You're part of the mounted police family," he said matter-of-factly. "I took a smoked brisket over to Mason's for the party. Lily was having a fit about something, so I came without him." He pointed to the restroom door. "Go ahead and wash up. I'll bring the kit."

One look in the mirror explained Cruz's consternation.

Dirt and dried blood streaked down her face. The cut on her forehead, above her right eyebrow, was about an inch wide. There was a scrape under her chin. She removed her coat and gingerly massaged her shoulder. Although it ached deep in the joint, she was able to move it without severe pain.

Cruz returned with the kit, his body filling the doorway. "Need anything else?"

"A hug and a promise this isn't going to happen again."

"I don't make promises I can't keep. Not anymore. As for the other—" Clearing his throat, he stepped forward and started to lift his arms.

She put her hand on his chest and, feeling his muscles flex, jerked it away. Heat entered her cheeks. "I didn't mean for you to actually…"

"Right." The tips of his ears turned red, and he ducked his head to knead the back of his neck. "I'll be in Bell's office."

He spun on his heel and walked away. Jade shut the door and made a face at her reflection. "Why did you say that, to him of all people?"

She quickly washed her face, neck and hands and placed a bandage on her cut. Without a comb, there wasn't much she could do about her bird's nest hair. Her coat was dirty, with bits of mulch attached, but it was in one piece. Good thing, since she couldn't afford to buy another. This one was her backup.

She rejoined the men, who stood up. "Did you locate the truck?"

Bell nodded. "Abandoned at the dump entrance. Our guys are searching the surrounding area as we speak, but we're at a disadvantage without a physical description."

"I'll take you to the co-op for your vehicle," Cruz said.

"We'll inquire about security cameras while we're there. Maybe we'll get a glimpse of this guy."

The inside of Cruz's truck was immaculate. Of course, he didn't have a young child who liked to travel with toys and snacks. The newer model had heated seats, and she sank into the cushion with a sigh.

His radio was tuned to a country station, and a husky voice crooned about lost love. He punched the knob with his finger, blanketing the cab in silence. "Bell told me you jumped out of a moving vehicle."

"I didn't have a choice."

"I can think of a few seasoned officers who wouldn't have done what you did."

Pleasure spread through her at his admiring tone. "I'm all Henry has."

"What about his father?"

Axel's face flashed in her mind, and she grimaced. The drugs had inhibited her judgment. If she'd been thinking clearly, she wouldn't have stayed with him. "He's not part of our lives."

"Could he be behind these attacks?"

"What? No, he's—" She stopped short, having almost blurted the truth. Axel not only thought she was dead, he was also locked up.

Cruz arched a brow as he turned into the co-op lot.

"He doesn't want anything to do with us, trust me."

Axel didn't know about Henry. She'd wondered how he'd react to the knowledge he had a son. He wasn't capable of compassion or selflessness. However, he was the king of exploiting people. He'd use Henry as a pawn to get his own way, if given the chance.

A police cruiser was parked beside the main co-op entrance, the same one she'd entered earlier believing the danger had passed. How wrong she'd been. Cruz stayed close as they walked inside, his eyes alert and his mouth grim. She wished he'd put his hand on her back again. Returning here so soon after her ordeal was creating a serious attack of nerves.

Gary's greeting was different this time around. He looked spooked. The officer left the payment counter and met them near the shopping carts.

"The clerk didn't see or hear anything. They do have security cameras, but not in the warehouse area where Ms. Harris was abducted. I'm going to review the footage to see if we can spot him elsewhere on the property."

Cruz thanked him. "Jade, take me through what happened."

"I came to buy greenery for the vet clinic, so I grabbed a cart and headed this way." She retraced her steps, and he kept pace beside her.

"Were there any other customers or employees?"

"Just Gary."

Her heart rate picked up as they entered the designated aisle. Her cart was there, with her purse, and the final wreath she'd chosen was angled between the bottom shelf and cement floor. Those terrible moments rose up to torment her. Cruz walked to the end of the aisle, turning in a slow circle, obviously considering her abductor's approach and retreat. Had he dragged her from the building? Carried her over his shoulder?

She shuddered. Who was this man? Why had he targeted her?

And when would he strike next?

Cruz's thoughts were jumping around like hot grease on a skillet. He didn't like that Jade's attacker was acting with escalating boldness. A crowded public event was one thing. The hustle and bustle and cloak of darkness had acted in his favor. A store in the middle of town, in broad daylight, carried more risk.

Unable to quell his concern, he flipped the steaks he was grilling, then removed them to a plate. Mason opened the door for him. He appreciated the shift from chilled, pine-scented air to the warmth of Mason and Tessa's farmhouse kitchen. The tangy, smoky smell emanating from the plate he carried mingled with the aroma of fresh-baked sourdough loaves and made his stomach rumble with anticipation. As Cruz slid the plate in between sweet potato casserole and macaroni and cheese, his ears picked up Jade's velvet-soft voice.

He shifted to search the adjacent living room and watched as she boosted first Lily and then Henry up to hang their homemade ornaments on the tree. Her movements were stiff, and she was favoring her right shoulder. She hadn't told him she'd injured it. His gut said she hadn't told him a lot of things.

After leaving the co-op, he'd followed her home so she could change clothes and comb the debris from her hair. Now her green sweater deepened the color of her eyes, and her hair hung in a shimmering pearl curtain to the middle of her back. The bandage above her eye spoiled the illusion of holiday cheer.

He turned back to Mason. "What do you know about Jade's past?"

He scratched his beard. "Not much. Why?"

Cruz peeled the aluminum foil off the brisket and got a waft of steam. "She was evasive about her family. Clammed up when I asked about Henry's father." He hadn't exactly given her a reason to confide in him, though, had he? He hadn't gone out of his way to be a friendly neighbor.

"I figured she'd gotten burned." Mason studied her, his dark eyes contemplative. "She's close to Leslie and her family. Hasn't spoken about her own. I've sensed deep rifts. She's a compassionate person. Sensitive. Trauma would affect her deeply and make it difficult to discuss."

Cruz began to slice the meat. He couldn't shake the feeling that Jade was being intentionally deceptive. He'd developed a radar for that sort of thing while working with the Texas narcotics unit. He'd gone undercover to ferret out the men who'd killed his big brother, Sal, and had rubbed elbows with liars, thieves and murderers.

"Is she capable of hiding her child from his own father? Could she be a noncustodial parent on the run?"

"No."

There was a whole lot of conviction in his sergeant's voice. The notion was far-fetched, but it wasn't impossible. A burst of laughter brought his attention to her once more, and he saw her shaking her head at something Henry was saying. Her disquiet had temporarily dissolved, and she looked as she usually did—as serene and inviting as his favorite childhood swimming hole.

That scene in the station flooded back, and his chest burned where she'd touched him. He'd almost held her. Women had flirted and cajoled and tried to rope him, and he'd had no problem rebuffing them. One request from Jade Harris had him reaching for her. She'd certainly looked in desperate need of a hug, but she'd merely been venting her frustration.

Tessa, who'd retreated upstairs a while ago, returned to the kitchen. She walked with less than her usual pep, her watery gaze riveted on Mason. At his raised brows, she shook her head and walked into his waiting arms, resting her cheek in the curve of his neck. He whispered into her ear and stroked her back.

Concern kicked him in the ribs. When Tessa joined Jade and the kids, he glanced at Mason. "Is she okay?"

He shoved his hands in his pockets, his expression pensive. "She will be."

If Cruz thought the Lord would heed his pleas, he'd say a prayer for the couple. They'd walked through fire to get to where they were today, and he hated to think they were facing more trouble. Tessa and Jade embraced. Did Jade know what was going on?

Silver Williams and his wife, Lindsey, arrived with their arms full of gifts. Although they'd married in February, they still had the honeymoon glow. Had he and Denise ever looked at each other like that? Their marriage had imploded before their first anniversary, so he kind of doubted it. When Raven and her new husband, Aiden, arrived a short time later, Cruz experienced a familiar and unwelcome pinch of envy. Their unit dynamics had changed dramatically. He didn't belong to anyone. Hadn't in a long time. He'd convinced himself he liked it that way, because he'd tried commitment and failed. But now that his three partners were married, he was reevaluating his bachelor life.

Raven leaned past him to get a whiff of the brisket. "Smells delicious, Cruz. I'm starving."

Her joy had been on full display ever since Aiden had resurfaced, and Cruz couldn't be happier for her.

He handed her a small slice. She popped it in her mouth and made a humming noise. "Any progress on Jade's case?"

"Not yet." Last night, he'd been positive her attack was a random event. He'd even convinced her of it. If the stranger had been successful today, the blame would fall squarely on Cruz's shoulders.

A knowing tension entered Raven's face. "I thought the trouble was over for good."

Their unit had been bombarded with personal trials lately. Although Jade wasn't a mounted police officer, she was important to them. They wouldn't stand by and let her face danger on her own.

Tessa walked over and assessed the spread. "Grab a plate, everyone." She pointed to the plates and silverware on the counter. "We'll do this buffet-style."

The distressed white table situated between the island and patio doors was decorated with greenery and white candles. He'd helped Mason put in the extensions in order to have enough space.

The kids raced over, and Henry tugged on Cruz's shirt. "I want to sit next to you, Mr. Cruz."

He gently ruffled the boy's hair. "You got it, buddy."

Henry also wanted to sit beside Lily, which left Cruz in between the boy and his mother. Of course, Mason asked for everyone to hold hands during the prayer. It was tradition. Jade avoided his gaze as she slipped hers into his. A blush splashed across her cheeks. Cruz's focus swerved away from her and landed on Silver. He was watching them, his violet eyes speculative. His gray brows lifted a fraction, and a goading smile tipped his lips.

Cruz glared, hoping to forestall an inquisition later. The man had a way of pushing his buttons, much like a sibling would. Like Sal used to. The grief wasn't as breath-stealing as it used to be, but he felt his older brother's absence deep inside, like a wound that never healed.

Mason asked Aiden to do the honors, and the architecture professor happily agreed. As they prayed, Cruz found himself distracted by Henry's wiggling on his left and Jade's utter stillness on his right. He liked the way her hand fit into his, her fingers wrapped around his in a trusting way.

Conversation erupted around him as everyone began to dig in. Jade leaned close.

"Would you prefer to switch places with me? Henry will need some help."

He'd eaten enough meals with Mason, Tessa and Lily to know how it worked. "I'll manage."

"You're sure?"

"This ain't my first rodeo," he said, winking.

Her lashes swept down as her cheeks pinked. He could've kicked himself. If Silver or the others caught the exchange, he'd be in for it. He stuffed a roll in his mouth and turned to Henry, expecting to have to cajole him into eating his vegetables. He had no idea what sort of meals Jade prepared. He'd never given her personal habits and preferences much thought before today. But Henry tucked into the array of choices on his plate. Score for Jade.

The conversation touched on the literacy tutoring center Raven had opened and Aiden's return to teaching college students. They avoided the topic at the forefront of their minds—the attacks on Jade—out of consideration of the children. It wasn't long before Henry and Lily lost interest in their meals and scampered back to their makeshift craft table close to the tree.

Cruz received a phone call and excused himself. When he returned, everyone looked at him with questions in their eyes. He zeroed in on Jade. "The suspect's in the wind, and the security footage didn't capture anything useful. I'm sorry."

Her gaze darted to Henry. Her son was always her first thought, wasn't he?

Lindsey tossed her napkin beside her plate. "So what are we going to do to keep Jade safe?"

Everyone looked to him for direction. Why did they assume he was taking point on this?

FIVE

Ironic how a group of police officers had come to her defense the moment she encountered trouble. In her former life, she'd been the suspect. The guilty one.

Beside her, Cruz shifted in his chair, and she realized they were waiting for him to impart a brilliant plan of action. Was it because they were neighbors? Were the others under the impression that he and Jade interacted on a regular basis?

"Our suspect pool is empty." He turned to her. It took effort to concentrate on the words coming out of his mouth instead of how handsome he looked in his red-and-white-plaid shirt. "Has anyone come to mind? I was originally thinking tourist, but this second attack changes things. A majority of victims know their attackers."

Mason sprinkled salt and pepper on a second helping of potatoes. "What about the vet clinic? Is there a client whose behavior toward you has recently changed?"

She mentally ran down the short list of men in her life who made her uneasy. "Jeremiah Taylor. He's pestered me for months to go out with him. I was nice in the beginning, but then I had to get firm. His manner turned icy after that, bordering on rude."

"He's in the singles class at church, right?" Tessa said,

tucking her curls behind her ear. "You mentioned him a time or two. I haven't crossed paths with him very often. We sit in different sections during the service, and afterward I'm off to pick up Lily. Mason, does he have history with the police?"

"Not that I'm aware of."

Beside her, Cruz's hand fisted on his thigh. Their knees brushed, and her stomach tightened. Having all his scrutiny and intensity focused on her at close range was unsettling.

"Has he threatened you, Jade?"

"Not in so many words." She twisted the paper napkin into a tight roll. "I don't want to cause trouble for him if he's innocent."

"We'll be subtle. If we find anything linking him to the attacks, then there will be trouble."

His gaze promised retribution for hurting her. Why did he care about what happened to her all of a sudden? Why did her heart leap with anticipation every time he came close?

"You and Henry are welcome to stay with us until this guy is caught," Lindsey said, nudging her glasses farther up her nose.

"Or us," Raven chimed in, waving a hand between her and Aiden. "Although we don't have an indoor pool to offer." She winked at Silver.

"Nor do you have Lindsey's baking skills," he added, grinning.

"You're welcome here, too," Tessa said with feeling. "We have plenty of space."

Jade was overcome with gratitude, and it took her a few moments to speak. "Thank you. For now, I'd like to stay put and not upset Henry's routine."

Mason and Tessa were dealing with a serious issue,

and the other two couples were practically newlyweds. She couldn't bring herself to accept their offers. Besides, this guy had tried twice and been foiled twice. He had to know he'd gotten law enforcement's attention. Surely, he'd abandon his plan in order to stay out of jail.

"Who's ready for dessert? I brought peppermint brownies and cranberry-orange shortbread cookies." Lindsey scooted back her chair and popped to her feet. She immediately put her hand to her forehead and swayed. Silver shot out of his chair and caught her as she slumped sideways.

"Lindsey!" Worry reflected in Silver's eyes. "Guys, she's unconscious."

Everyone abandoned their seats. Jade remained on the fringe of the group, heart pounding with dread. Cruz helped Silver ease her to the floor, taking a pillow from Mason to slide beneath her head. "Has this happened before?"

"She's been having blood sugar issues lately." Silver's jaw was tight as he knelt beside her and checked her pulse. "Sometimes feels light-headed."

Aiden put his hand on Raven's shoulder. "Should I call an ambulance?"

Before anyone could answer, Lindsey's lashes fluttered behind her lenses. "No ambulance."

Silver had a tight grip on her hand. "How are you feeling, Linds?"

"Other than a slight headache, fine and dandy." She started to sit up, and Silver curved his arm around her shoulders.

"Take it easy."

She belatedly noticed everyone huddled around her. "I'm fine, I promise."

"We'll let the doctor have the final say on that. We're going to the walk-in clinic."

"But dessert—"

He kissed her lightly on the lips. "They'll save you some."

"I want one of each, Tessa. Don't let the guys eat all of your coconut cream pie, either."

Silver kept her tucked close to his side as they made their way outside.

After dessert, Tessa suggested they postpone the gift exchange until a later date, and everyone pitched in clearing the dishes and storing leftovers. By the time they were done, exhaustion settled heavily on Jade's shoulders. She'd need a good night's rest if she was going to tackle the patient load tomorrow with a clear head.

"I'm going home, Tess. Keep me updated."

Tessa's hazel eyes assessed her. "Are you sure you don't want to stay here tonight?"

"Positive."

"I'll come with you and check things out," Cruz said, washing and drying his hands.

Jade didn't argue, partly because she didn't have the energy and partly because she would feel safer knowing he'd cleared the house. Henry wasn't ready to leave, but his protests died down when he learned Cruz was coming, too. He clearly liked the officer, and she worried that he'd get ideas. He'd been asking why he didn't have a father like Lily and his other friend Kai, and she'd struggled to find a suitable answer that would satisfy him.

The sun was on its downward slide when they parked in her driveway. Cruz came to her truck window and got her keys. A few minutes later, he emerged from the house and gave her a thumbs-up. He waited on the porch for them. Henry hopped along the pavers and up the steps.

"Catch me, Mr. Cruz!"

He jumped, and Cruz caught him and swung him up into his arms with a laugh. "Aren't you tired yet, cowboy?"

He shook his head with fervor, wavy locks falling into his eyes. "Can we ride Gunsmoke?"

"Not tonight." His gaze landed on Jade. "Your mom has had a busy weekend, and she needs her rest."

A lump formed in Jade's throat. How wonderful it would be to have a partner who looked out for her best interests, who supported her on the hard days and made her laugh when she took life too seriously. A man who'd be a good role model for Henry and would love him as much as she did.

"Why does she need rest?"

"She has to work tomorrow, and so do I. You're on school break, so all you have to do tomorrow is play."

"Sometimes I stay at Lily's house and sometimes Kai's."

"Good deal. You get to play with different toys."

"Kai has a ball pit."

The pair looked comfortable, like a real father and son. Cruz didn't seem to mind Henry's natural exuberance.

Cruz smiled at Henry, and his features went from handsome to breath-stealing. His gaze shifted to her, temporarily including her in his good humor.

She felt a pang of sharp disappointment.

To love and cherish someone required honesty. As long as she was playacting at life, she didn't have her whole heart to give.

Cruz Castillo had been on Jade's mind when she'd fallen asleep and when she'd woken up. Probably because Henry wouldn't stop talking about him. Now she was in his workplace, ears straining to detect his deep, smooth voice, turning at every sound to see if he was nearby. Thanks to her unusual weekend, she'd forgotten about the clinic's scheduled visit to the mounted police stables.

Would Cruz stick to his normal routine and steer clear

of her? It would be best if he did. Mooning over a police officer was the definition of foolishness.

"Four down, two to go." One of Jade's bosses, Dr. Belinda Lisle, gestured to Lightning's stall. "I'll tackle this big guy."

Jade smiled, pleased Belinda had let her have Renegade. He was the largest of all their horses and, in her opinion, the most likely to grace a magazine cover. He could be mischievous and rambunctious but also sweet.

Inside his stall, she set her supplies down and greeted him. "There's my handsome guy. How have you been? Missed me?" She rubbed his nose, and he bobbed his head. "It's time for your deworming and shots. I promise I'll be quick."

"Told you he was your favorite."

Jade whipped her head around, her stomach jumping. "Cruz."

He entered the stall and stood next to her, his attention on his equine partner. She detected his pleasing cologne amid the myriad smells of horseflesh, hay and leather. He wore the same informal uniform as the other officers—a collared, long-sleeve navy shirt, featuring the Serenity Mounted Police emblem, tucked into black utility pants. Unlike the military-style boots the others favored, Cruz sported his cowboy boots.

He reached to stroke Renegade's neck, and his shoulder muscles bunched beneath the fabric. "Did you get any rest last night?"

She was distracted, studying his neat goatee and how it accentuated his cheekbones and square jaw. Would it be soft or prickly? He turned his head and caught her staring.

She averted her gaze. "I did, thank you."

He'd made her promise to call him if she felt scared or

anxious. He'd also had her text him when she left the house and when she arrived at the clinic.

She cleared her throat and went to work, hoping he'd return to his. But he stayed and watched, muscular arms crossed over his chest, as she cleaned Renegade's neck with alcohol in preparation for the injection.

"And Henry?"

"He wasn't cranky when he woke up this morning, so I'm guessing he slept well. You should know that you're his favorite topic at the moment. Although I didn't have much information to impart."

His mouth eased into a smile. "Is that so? You can tell him I grew up on a horse and goat ranch near Bandera, Texas."

"Are your folks still there?"

"My parents and younger brother, Diego. He's taken over most of the day-to-day operations."

She heard pride and maybe a little longing in his voice. "Ranching wasn't your calling?"

"I used to think I'd live and die on that ranch. My priorities shifted, and I decided law enforcement was it for me."

She removed the cap and checked the needle. Inserting it, she pulled back to check for blood. Seeing none, she injected the solution and then massaged the muscles.

"Did you work with a mounted police unit in Texas?"

"Narcotics. I did multiple undercover stints."

Of course he had. Jade didn't want to hear about it. Memories of those days made her cringe inside. Even though she knew Jesus had forgiven her for her sins, she couldn't help feeling sad about the things she'd done.

After dosing Renegade with the dewormer paste, she didn't linger. Cruz followed her into the wide aisle. Belinda was already walking toward the offices. "I'm going to speak to Mason. Meet you at the truck."

When the veterinarian was no longer within hearing range, Cruz said, "Does she know about the attacks?"

"Seems everyone knows." One of the downsides to living in a small town, she'd learned.

"She's obviously okay with you working."

"Why wouldn't she be?"

"Officers Bell and Weiland spoke with Jeremiah Taylor this morning. He adamantly denies involvement. While he doesn't have anyone to substantiate his whereabouts on Saturday night, he has a rock-solid alibi for Sunday afternoon. Multiple people have verified he wasn't at the co-op."

Jade's hopes that this would be solved quickly evaporated. "What now?"

He tugged on his earlobe. "You think of anyone else, you let us know. Until then, don't let your guard down."

"You think he'll come after me again?"

"I can't rule it out."

"Cruz, I'm your neighbor. Your horse's favorite vet tech. Level with me."

His chest expanded on a sigh. "He's taken big risks trying to get to you. To answer your question, I suspect he won't be swayed from his goals."

Despite the balmy warmth of the stables, cold swept through Jade. Her phone vibrated. "It's Elaine. Henry's at her house today. I have to take it."

He nodded and started to step away.

"Hey, Elaine. What's up?"

"A man was here, at the house. O-outside. Kai and Henry were playing in the tree fort, and I noticed him in the field." Her voice was high and wobbly.

Jade's heart slammed against her ribs. "The boys. Where are they?"

Cruz pivoted back, brows lowered.

"In the kitchen. They're safe. I may have overreacted, but after what happened to you..." She trailed off, and Jade could almost see her friend twisting her auburn hair into knots.

"You did the right thing, Elaine. Is he still there?"

"I don't know."

"I'm coming over." She ended the call.

"What is it?"

"There was a man in the vacant field behind her house. He was watching the boys." She walked as fast as her wobbly legs would take her. He fell into step beside her. "I have to see Henry. Make sure he's okay."

She found Belinda in Mason's office and explained the situation.

"Let's go back to the clinic so you can get your truck," Jade's boss said.

She clenched her teeth. The clinic was in the opposite direction of Elaine's. Returning there would delay her by at least thirty minutes.

Mason pushed out of his chair and opened his mouth.

Cruz spoke first. "The paperwork on my desk can wait a while. I'll take her."

Jade wasn't sure how she refrained from hugging him.

Jade's nervous energy radiated in waves through the cab. Her hands were in constant motion, twisting, furling, splaying, palms rubbing over her hot-pink scrub pants. He extended his arm across the bench seat and rested his hand on her shoulder, hoping to impart comfort. The only acknowledgment of his gesture was a hard swallow. She kept her eyes on the leafless trees, brownish-green grass and brittle blue sky, probably calculating the remaining distance based on familiar landmarks.

They didn't know who this stranger was or why he

was on Elaine's property. But Cruz wasn't discounting anything.

He wanted to see for himself that Henry was okay. Besides, he was the only one with a free morning. Mason had a lunch date with Tessa—and they clearly needed uninterrupted time together. Silver had accompanied Lindsey to the lab for bloodwork. Raven was trying to hire more tutors for the literacy center.

It occurred to him that no one depended on him outside this job—besides Gunsmoke and Old Bob.

He gave her shoulder a squeeze. "Hey."

She seemed to remember she wasn't alone. Pushing her hair behind her ear, she looked at him. The stark fear in her eyes was like a kick in the stomach. He didn't have to be a father to imagine the thoughts and emotions she was dealing with. Twice in the span of two days, she'd been violently attacked, and now she suspected this man had switched his sights to her only child.

He glanced between her and the road. "Henry is sitting at Elaine's kitchen table, probably eating Popsicles or cookies or something else he wouldn't normally be eating for a midmorning snack. He's fine."

She nodded slowly, trying to hold tightly to his reassurance. "Elaine does keep a secret stash for when the boys get too rambunctious."

"How did you and Elaine become friends?" He had to distract her from her musings.

"Story hour."

"I don't know what that is."

"The library has story hour for the kids every Saturday. A librarian reads them a book. Sometimes it's followed by a craft. Kai and Henry got on well together, and Elaine and I began chatting. We scheduled a playdate, and it became a regular thing." She leaned forward, the seat belt digging into her shoulder. "There's her road."

Cruz made the turn and shifted his focus to their surroundings. Elaine and her husband, Franklin, lived on a quiet lane. The homes sat on several-acre plots. Some were wooded, and some were gently rolling fields dotted with cattle. They were closer to the foot of the mountains here, and the high, rounded ridges—brown and dark this time of year—hemmed them in. Because it was a Monday morning, many of the homeowners were at work. There was little activity that he could see.

The Latimer home was the fifth one down, and Jade unbuckled as he reached the drive. She bailed before he could switch off the engine. He hurried to catch up with her. The front door of the stately brick home opened, and Elaine ushered them inside.

"Did you see anyone?" Her complexion wan, she rolled the hem of her shirt and released it. The material was wrinkled from what he guessed was constant bunching. "I've been watching from the windows and haven't seen him again."

"There wasn't anyone on the road," Jade told her, craning her neck toward the kitchen.

Elaine gestured behind her. "They're working on a puzzle."

They progressed across the tile floor through the living room and around a corner to the kitchen, which spanned the rear wall. The boys were side by side on the table's bench seat, heads together as they considered the puzzle pieces. Empty pudding cups had been pushed to the side.

When Henry spied Jade, his face lit up. "Mommy!"

He scrambled off the bench and threw his arms around her waist. Jade bent over and returned the hug. Her hair swung forward like an ivory silk curtain, enveloping them in their own safe world. Cruz had a feeling she would've preferred to hold her son longer, but Henry squirmed out of her hold. Her eyes were suspiciously bright when she straightened.

"Look at our puzzle, Mr. Cruz."

Cruz moved behind Kai and Henry and inspected their work. "Good job, boys."

"Franklin's at a dentist appointment this morning," Elaine informed Cruz. "I tried to reach him, but his phone's turned off. He listed a bicycle for sale, and I thought maybe he'd arranged for someone to come out and look at it. But most people would come to the door, not just wander around the property. Plus, the guy was fixated on the boys. It occurred to me that it could be the same man who…" Her voice trailed off, obviously not wanting to continue out of consideration for the children.

"What did he look like?" Jade asked, smoothing her hands over her bright scrub shirt. Now that she'd seen Henry for herself, she seemed more in command of her emotions.

"Tall. Muscular. He had a baseball hat on, so I couldn't make out his features or hair color."

"What about clothing?" Cruz asked.

"Um, jeans, I think. Tan shirt with a picture on the front."

"Are you in contact with your closest neighbors?"

"I have their numbers."

"Call them."

While she did that, Jade paced between the windows. He was about to tell her to move away when Elaine spoke.

"The Griggses aren't home. Betsy Campbell is, though, and she hasn't noticed anyone lurking around."

"I'm going to take a look around outside."

Elaine explained the layout of the property. He walked

the length and breadth of it, searching for footprints or other clues left behind. The warehouse garage was set back from the house, some distance away from the in-ground pool. The garage doors were open—an invitation for mischief in Cruz's mind.

There was a red fishing boat on a trailer in the first bay and a Chevy Silverado in the second. The third bay was empty. Silver utility shelves and red tool cabinets lined the side walls. There was valuable equipment sitting around, and none of it looked disturbed. He spied a door and wondercd if it led to a storage closet or outside.

He turned the knob, nudged it open with his boot and caught sight of paint cans and cardboard boxes. The hairs on the back of his neck stood to attention, and he tensed.

Something heavy connected with his skull, and excruciating pain ripped a moan from his throat. He stumbled into the room, his knees refusing to support him, and slammed into the concrete. His breath wheezed from his lungs. He tried to reach his gun and earned another blow to the middle of his back before he could. Shadows danced at the edge of his vision.

Something clattered to the floor, followed by retreating footsteps. The perp was getting away—and he could be heading straight for Jade and Henry.

SIX

Out of habit, Cruz reached for his radio to call for backup. But he wasn't in his official uniform. It took immense effort to get to his feet. As soon as the swirling sensation passed, he gave chase, pulling his phone from his pocket and contacting dispatch. His aching skull screamed in protest, and his stomach threatened mutiny. Gritting his teeth, he flew by the boat, only to stumble to a stop before sprinting into the open.

Get a grip on yourself, man. Unholstering his weapon, he checked his sight lines while maintaining cover and spotted the suspect fleeing toward the neighbor's woods. Not going for Jade, then. Good.

His pace wasn't fast or efficient. The perp put increasing distance between them and ducked into the woods. Moments later, Cruz heard an engine rev. Sounded like an off-road motorcycle. He slowed as he entered the woods. He wasn't going to catch up with him, but at least he could give patrol a description.

There was a flash of blue and white between the trees, and then nothing.

A frustrated growl rumbled through his chest. Returning his weapon to its holster, he jogged back the way he'd come. The women must've been watching from the windows, because Jade was waiting by the door.

"You should take the boys upstairs," he grunted, adrenaline wearing off and pain demanding to make its presence known.

Her green eyes went wide as, chest heaving, he leaned against the wall. He was trying not to pass out.

"Elaine?" Jade spoke her friend's name without looking at her.

The other woman hustled over to the table. "Boys, let's go play LEGOs."

"What about our puzzle?" Kai asked.

Cruz closed his eyes and focused on drawing air in and letting it out. When Jade took his hand, he reopened them and found they were alone.

"Sit down before you fall over." He allowed her to lead him to a chair at the table and gently push him into it. "Where are you hurt?"

"Head. Back."

She moved behind him. Leaning close, she lightly parted his hair, her fingers gentle. "You're bleeding, and a knot is already forming." Her hands rested on his shoulders, and he was tempted to lean against her. "What did he hit you with?"

"A metal bar of some sort. We'll test it for fingerprints."

"I'm concerned about a possible concussion." As she listed off the symptoms, she bent her head forward and her hair tickled his ear. "I'm going to lift your shirt."

He tensed as her fingers trailed across his back, just below the line of pain. He couldn't remember the last time he'd been treated with such tenderness, and uncomfortable emotion filled him. Instead of analyzing it, he homed in on the anger he felt toward the man who was targeting an innocent woman and child.

"His hair was black."

He stood up, needing distance between them. His head swam for a moment.

"What?" She looked at him quizzically.

"Our guy. His hat was knocked sideways by a branch, and I saw his hair. It's black. Cut short. There's a tattoo on his right forearm, but I was too far away to make out the details."

His phone pressed to his ear, he updated dispatch and strode to the front porch to await the patrol units. He breathed deeply of the brisk air, hoping it would clear his head.

Jade followed him. "I'll go with you to the hospital if you'd like."

"Hospital?"

She held his gaze. "Your injuries need to be checked out."

Mason would come to the same conclusion. He took the welfare of his officers seriously. "Later. Right now, I have a dangerous criminal to catch."

Jade dropped her keys on the kitchen counter, opened the overhead cabinet door and pointed to her selection of herbal teas. "Want some?"

Raven smiled and lifted her monogrammed travel mug. "I've got coffee."

Henry's high-pitched singing carried from his bedroom, and the officer's smile widened. Raven and Mason had converged on Elaine's not long after the patrol officers arrived. Cruz had jumped into the front seat of Officer Bell's cruiser, and they'd taken off...but not before he'd rolled down his window and basically ordered Raven to accompany Jade home.

Jade selected her tea. "Will you make sure Cruz sees a doctor?"

Raven leaned against the counter and ran her hand along her braid. Her wedding rings winked in the afternoon sunlight streaming through the sink window. "Cruz has a stubborn streak, but Mason outranks him." She smirked. "He'll go."

Jade was surprised by the depth of her concern. Cruz had been a constant factor on the fringes of her life since she'd rented this house in Serenity several years ago. They may not have had much interaction, but she'd known he was next door in case of an emergency. He was a visible presence around town, strong and tall in Renegade's saddle, ready to protect Serenity's citizens. She'd seen him in action. Once, he'd chased a robbery suspect through the square and, leaping from the saddle, tackled the man to the ground. In a matter of seconds, Cruz had had the man in handcuffs.

She'd begun to think of him as invincible. When he'd come inside at Elaine's, she'd been alarmed by his pallor and the weakness he'd allowed her to see.

Raven must've guessed the direction of her thoughts, because she said, "Don't worry. It would take a lot to derail that tough-as-nails cowboy."

She filled the kettle with water. "Do you think they'll find this man?"

"Hard to say. There are lots of secluded coves, trails and wooded areas for him to hide in. Even an outsider would find it easy to slip away."

Jade chose a mug and got out the honey while the water heated. She would reach out to Alan Prescott again. This time, she'd make sure to relay the details. When she'd received Elaine's phone call that morning, she'd had the fleeting, terrifying thought that Axel might've escaped prison. But Axel had auburn hair, not black, and he'd avoided tattoos, saying they made it too easy for cops to identify him. Not to mention Prescott would've alerted her to any trouble. If Axel had somehow gotten out, the US Marshals would've swooped in and whisked her and Henry away.

The thought was incomprehensible. She'd put down roots here. She couldn't bear to imagine leaving her friends, her church, her job.

Raven consulted her watch. "I've got to get back to the stables."

Jade walked with her through the living room. Raven poked her head into Henry's room and told him goodbye. Henry stopped playing with his trains long enough to wave and smile shyly at the officer.

"You've done a wonderful job with him," the other woman told Jade.

Raven didn't stick around for her response, so she missed the tears gathering in Jade's eyes. *Thank You, Lord, for bringing me out of the pit I dug myself into. Thank You for Your salvation and that Your mercies are new every morning. Thank You for letting me be Henry's mom.*

She left another message for Prescott and attacked the never-ending laundry pile. Later that evening, she was preparing a salad and grilled chicken when her phone rang. Her heart performed a backflip when she saw Cruz's name on the screen.

"I'm afraid I don't have the news you wanted," he began without preamble. "One of our guys spotted the dirt bike leaving Serenity and heading toward Pigeon Forge. We're coordinating with their law enforcement agencies. The metal bar he used will be examined for trace evidence."

Disappointment leaked into her. "How are you feeling?"

"You'll be happy to know I went to the clinic. I've got a mild concussion, but I'm cleared to work."

Relieved, she considered inviting him for supper but dismissed the idea. She liked him and wanted to get to know him. But given all she was hiding, she had to keep her distance.

She heard talking in the background.

"I have to go, Jade. I'll be home in an hour or so. If you see anything suspicious or just feel like something's off, call me."

He hung up, and she stared off into space. Why did it seem natural for him to call her? And why did she have to stow her phone in the drawer to keep from texting him a supper invitation? It wasn't fair that the first man to capture her interest was a cop. She'd been on a total of maybe five dates in as many years. The prospect of being vulnerable made her twitchy. What if she chose the wrong man again? This time, she wouldn't be the only one to suffer.

After she and Henry finished eating, she stored the leftovers and settled him on the couch to watch *Frosty the Snowman*. She went to start another load of laundry and realized she was out of detergent. This house was charming but seriously lacking in storage. Her extra supplies had to be stored in the shed.

"I've got to get something from the shed, Henry. I'll be right back."

Nodding, he pulled his feet onto the cushion and propped his chin on his knees.

Out on the deck, she searched the yard and the pastures beyond the fence. Cruz's horses grazed nearby. Birds chirped and looped between the pine and the oak. From the top step, she could see a slice of Cruz's barn. His house was on the far side of that, however, so she couldn't know for sure if he was home or not.

Jade hurried across the yard. She entered the darkened shed and tripped over something just inside, catching herself on a stack of plastic bins. A foul smell unlike any she'd ever encountered wound around her, making her gag. Had a sick animal crawled in here and died? She turned to see what she'd tripped over, hoping a shovel or rake had fallen across the threshold. Hoping it wasn't a poor stray cat or dog.

Her blood turned to sludge. Was that a man's shoe?

Moving as if in slow motion, she took two steps closer and touched the foot with the tip of her tennis shoe.

It was real, all right. And unmoving.

Sweat rolling between her shoulder blades, she crouched and lifted the blue tarp. Then she screamed.

SEVEN

Cruz never made it into the barn. He dropped the sack of carrots in the dirt and sprinted for Jade's the minute she called him.

"Dead body," she'd said, her panic practically reaching through the speaker to claw at his throat. "In my shed."

"Are you safe?"

"I—I think so. Henry's in the house."

He passed a giant magnolia tree in the field between his barn and her house. "Almost there," he told her now. "Stay on the line."

"Okay."

He heard her talking to Henry, urging him to stay inside. He pushed between two Douglas firs and emerged in her well-tended yard. The evergreens flanking the backyard created a dark green vista, and her pink scrubs stood out like a brilliant summer bloom. She leaned against the shed, one arm hugging her middle and the other hand flat against her mouth. Her eyes were large in her pale face, and they fastened onto him with relief and a hefty helping of trust.

She lifted her fingers a fraction. "Behind the door. Under the tarp."

Cruz entered, careful to disturb as little as possible in

this crime scene. The stench was enough to make him re-think that day-old burrito he'd scarfed down a few minutes ago. He eyed the victim's leather shoe. Good quality, prac-tically new. Lifting the tarp, he unleashed another wave of powerful, eye-watering odor. Cruz noted crucial details—plain clothing, wedding ring, expensive watch. Male, short brown hair. Dried blood and such heavy bruising a facial ID would be impossible. No obvious method of death.

After summoning assistance from dispatch, he stepped outside. Jade sprang away from the wall as if it seared her.

"Who is he? What if Henry had discovered him?" She gasped. "Were we home when it happened?"

Cruz settled his hands on her shoulders and ducked his head to be closer to her eye level. "Breathe, Jade. Close your eyes and breathe."

She instantly obeyed. Then her eyes popped open, and she grimaced. "All I can see is his face. His features are beyond recognition."

Her body was trembling. Shucking off his jacket, he draped it over her shoulders and turned her toward a black metal bench near the base of one of the live oaks. "Let's go sit for a minute."

Guiding her over, he waited until she'd gotten settled be-fore crouching in front of her, one knee in the crisp grass. She anticipated his questions, because she launched into a play-by-play of her evening, even mentioning almost in-viting him over for supper. Had she meant to reveal that detail? The admission startled and intrigued him to the point he had to ask her to repeat a few things.

Corralling his unruly thoughts, he studied her. Her pulse flittered in her neck. Her gestures were erratic, her hands not quite steady. Her alarm was genuine. Anyone would be unnerved by a deceased person on their property. But why did he have a feeling she knew more than she was letting on? Was she somehow involved?

He would be remiss in his duty if he didn't consider the last three days' events from all angles. While he trusted Mason and Tessa's judgment, what did any of them really know about Jade? It would be easy to believe she was as pure as the driven snow, with her guileless green eyes and angelic features, framed by that glorious white-blond hair.

She'd wanted him to sit at her table and share a homemade meal with her and her son.

If she *had* invited him, what would've been his response?

Cruz stood. "I'm going to look around."

Her brow creased, tugging at the small bandage above her right eye. Her busted lower lip looked sore and tender. There were scratches and bruises on her neck. He reined in his suspicions. He would do well to focus on the villain who'd targeted her and whether or not this suspicious death was connected.

He approached the shed, surveying what he could see from a distance. If there were drag marks or footprints, he didn't want to disturb them. The patrol unit arrived with Detective York, who immediately set up a perimeter and peppered Jade with questions. Then he inspected the scene without touching the body. They had to wait for the medical examiner.

Standing beside Jade, Cruz saw her look toward the house. Henry was plastered against the glass door leading to the deck. The height and angle prevented him from seeing the shed—Cruz had checked.

Jade clutched the lapels of his jacket close to her throat. "I need to be with Henry."

"Gather your things," he found himself saying. "You two are staying with me tonight."

Her hands dropped to her side. "I don't know if that's such a good idea."

He arched a brow. "Will Henry sleep peacefully in there after seeing uniforms crawling over his yard? Will you?"

Her teeth came out to burrow in her lip, and she winced. "I'll get our things."

The headache he'd earned that morning had lessened throughout the day. It returned with greater intensity as he waited in the darkening yard. He could've contacted Mason or suggested she sleep at Elaine's. Probably should've. But she looked ready to drop from exhaustion—more mental than physical—and Henry's bedtime was fast approaching. Cruz had a perfectly adequate spare bedroom next door. There was no reason why he shouldn't offer them protection and a sense of security.

Detective York had told her not to leave town. His inscrutable look had made her uneasy. Did he suspect she'd had something to do with that man's death?

"I'm hungry, Mommy." Henry bounced on the bed in Cruz's guest room. His normal routine had been obliterated, and he was in a different house. He wasn't showing any signs of winding down for the night.

Jade pinched the bridge of her nose. She'd forgotten to pack a snack.

"I've got apples," Cruz said from the doorway.

She jerked, her heart thudding. "I didn't hear you come in."

He hadn't given them a tour. He'd shown them directly into this room, pointed out the bathroom and then hurried out to the barn.

He leaned against the doorjamb, hands in his pants pockets. Other than a streak of dirt across the chest of his official collared shirt, he looked pristine. His posture was relaxed. She sensed he was far from it. His eyes were watchful. Wary. Did he suspect her of foul play? What was his true motive for offering his home as refuge?

"Do you have peanut butter?" Henry hopped off the bed, sock-covered feet hitting the carpet with a thump.

Cruz was a bachelor accustomed to solitude at the end of his workday. How would he handle having an energetic child around?

He cocked his head to the side. "No, but I'm pretty sure I have peanut butter crackers. Will that do?"

Henry nodded and skipped past Cruz into the hallway.

Jade placed his pajamas on the bedside table. "He's usually not this energetic at night. I'm sorry if we're keeping you from something. Or someone."

One brow arched, and she blushed. She wasn't fishing for information. If Cruz Castillo had finally deigned to date a local woman, every Serenity resident would hear about it.

"I haven't had an overnight guest since Diego visited last year, so my skills are rusty. You'll have to speak up if you need something."

She recalled seeing the younger man around town. The Castillo men had similar golden-brown complexions and coal-black hair, only Cruz was taller and stockier.

"That won't be a problem for Henry. Most kids his age announce their wants and needs to anyone who will listen."

They went into the kitchen, where Henry was already taking inventory of Cruz's cabinet contents. Jade intervened, explaining why that wasn't considered good manners. Cruz smiled, seemingly unbothered by the intrusion.

"I like this color," she said, skimming the basil-green bottom cabinets. A stained wooden countertop ran the length of two walls and was offset by white subway tiles.

Matching wood shelves stood in for the upper cabinets. There was a generous island in the middle.

"The previous owner redid it before putting the house up for sale. I use the smoker and grill more than the appliances in here. As long as the kitchen functions, I'm happy."

He'd brought them in via the back door, and she'd glimpsed his outdoor-cooking setup on the deck.

"You use those year-round?"

"Pretty much."

He extracted a box of prepackaged crackers and set it on the island. Then he tapped a glass bowl piled high with apples and told Henry to pick one. Henry made his choice, and Cruz helped him wash it beneath the spray of water. Then he sliced it into fat quarters and arranged it on a plate.

His dark eyes flashed up, blunt fingers resting on the bowl. "Want one, Jade?"

She shook her head, unable to consider eating anything. "Just water."

He retrieved a glass and inclined his head toward the fridge dispenser. "Make yourself at home."

Henry asked to watch television. Because it would be futile to put him to bed yet, she got him settled on the couch while Cruz found children's programming. He returned to the kitchen, and she followed him.

"How long before we hear anything on the dead man?"

"Hard to say. And we can't build a list of suspects until we know the victim's identity." He tossed the apple core into the garbage and washed the knife. "Have you spoken to your landlord?"

"I have." Kevin had been understandably shocked. "He's probably over there now."

He dried off his hands and returned the knife to the butcher block. "He didn't have any meaningful information?"

"He's in the dark, like me."

His phone rang, and he glanced down at the screen. "That's Detective York now."

His responses were one syllable, so she didn't glean much from his side of the conversation. A strange expression gripped his features. When he ended the call, he stared at the screen for long moments, as if he was reluctant to look at her.

"They found a badge."

"An employee badge?"

His gaze finally lifted. His brown eyes could be at times warm and inviting. Other times, they were friendly but distant, warning her to keep her distance. Now, they were hot with confusion.

He shook his head. "US marshal."

Numbness entombed her. Could it be? No. *Please, Lord, no.*

But Prescott hadn't returned her messages. Her thoughts whirled, round and round, slamming against her skull.

She was tempted to slump to the floor until the weakness bled out of her body. The ramifications were too huge, too frightening to process.

"Jade?"

Most people wouldn't connect the seemingly random attacks with the death of a US marshal. Cruz was a seasoned officer with years of undercover work under his belt. His mind would go where others' wouldn't.

Somehow, she pushed all the emotions deep inside, imprisoning them. "That's terrible," she said, her voice sounding almost normal. "Do they know his name?"

"Not yet. His identification and credentials are missing." He stared hard at her, dissecting her reaction. "But they will."

She pressed her hand against her stomach, praying she

didn't throw up. "I, uh, am going to get Henry ready for bed. See you in the morning."

She pivoted on her heel, expecting him to forestall her. She didn't breathe freely until she and Henry were closed inside the guest bedroom.

If the downed marshal was Prescott, it could mean only one thing—her sweet life in Serenity had come to an end.

EIGHT

Restorative sleep was all but impossible. Jade got snatches of rest, but mostly she stared at the gleaming drapes on the windows. Her chest felt heavy, and she couldn't get the deceased marshal out of her mind. The wedding ring, specifically. He had a wife somewhere who was wondering why he hadn't come home. Did he have children?

Lord, did that man give his life trying to warn me?

Until his identity was confirmed, she couldn't know for sure.

Why else would he be here? Face it, Jade. Axel is at the root of this nightmare.

A great trembling started deep inside her and pulsed through her limbs. Had Axel pulled her into those woods? Had he followed her into the co-op, strangled her and tossed her into that dump truck?

The unanswered questions prevented her from sleeping. The moon's glow behind the sheer curtains gradually gave way to the pink blush of dawn. Unable to take the inactivity a minute longer, she eased out of bed and tucked the cover around Henry. She changed into the only outfit she'd packed—black pants, a white blouse printed with Dalmatians and a black sweater—and pulled a brush through her hair until her scalp tingled. She tiptoed along the hall, glad it was a split-bedroom floor plan. A confrontation with Cruz was inevitable. He'd want answers...and she had to figure out what those would be. Continue the charade or confess everything?

Jade punched in the alarm code he'd given her and, praying he was a heavy sleeper, stole outside. The scene was pretty enough to grace a calendar. Fog hugged the pastures. The red barn formed a dramatic backdrop for the trees' gnarled branches. Nearby ducks honked a morning serenade.

The barn blocked the view of her house. According to Cruz, the police would be there until every scrap of evidence had been collected...even if it took all night. She couldn't sleep and didn't want to wake Cruz. Why not check to see if a member of the crime scene unit was still there? Or a patrol officer? They might have valuable information.

She descended the stairs and strolled through the yard. When she reached the back side of the barn near the paddock, she noticed the freestanding lights had been removed and the yellow caution tape was intact. There weren't any voices or activity. Movement in her peripheral vision startled her. But it was only Gunsmoke coming to greet her.

She walked over to the slatted fence and ran her hand along the horse's face. "Good morning." There was a slight scar where she'd patched up a nasty cut he'd sustained last year.

He nudged her shoulder. "I suppose you think I'm out here to feed you, huh?" Spying Old Bob lumbering toward them, she gestured to the barn. "Meet me inside, boys."

Cruz had gone above and beyond for her. Crossing some of the chores off his list was the least she could do. Especially since he would probably refuse to speak to her once he learned the truth, much less provide protection.

Having treated both horses before, she was familiar with his tack and feed room setup. The horses ambled into their respective stalls, which had been left open to the pastures overnight. She measured out the sweet feed and dispensed it into their buckets.

Turning toward Gunsmoke's exit, she halted midstep. The bucket she held crashed to the dirt.

"Hello, Jenny."

His voice was raspier than she remembered. He was also larger than she remembered.

Axel had bulked up in prison. His sweatshirt stretched over his rough-hewn upper body, barely able to contain the overblown biceps and ropy neck muscles. He wouldn't need a weapon to subdue her.

"Like what you see?" His lips curled into a sneer, and his blue eyes were surly. His auburn hair had been dyed black, and it was shaved close to his head.

She darted toward the pasture opening. He blocked her, his meaty hand snagging her throat and shoving her up against the enclosure partition. His mouth crushed hers, and she whimpered. He smelled like alcohol, stale cigars and sweat.

Desperate to escape, she kneed his inner thigh. Axel growled and ripped his mouth from hers, glaring down at her. She braced herself for a blow that didn't come.

"Still feisty, I see." He suddenly laughed, tweaking her collar. "The clothing has changed, but inside you're the same street-savvy fireball."

"How did you find me?" Her heart quivered like a frightened rabbit.

"Your photograph was on the news." When she didn't respond, his brows inched up. "The kid who saved his little sister from a fire? The story is popular online. One of my guys saw it and got word to me."

The memory clicked into place. The story had been big news in Serenity. Several news outlets had come to town and featured the boy. She hadn't known she'd been caught on camera.

"How did you get out?"

His ire returned full force, and the pressure on her neck increased. "Took time and planning. A few bribes, too. While you were living it up here in Serenity, I was locked away in that cement box." His gaze blazed over her face. "I daydreamed about this reunion, you know. I thought of all the ways I'd end you. But watching you this week has changed my mind."

"You've been here a *week*?"

"I've learned patience, Jenny. I've also learned to be flexible. I don't believe I'll kill you. At least, not at first."

Her throat was so dry she couldn't speak.

"You've created a prim and proper life for yourself and your son. We both know it's a sham. I'm going to enjoy stripping it away. Everything you think you gained by turning on me will be gone with one slide of the needle." He snapped his fingers near her ear, and she flinched.

Then his words registered. She shook her head from side to side. Denial was a sour taste in her mouth.

With his free hand, he traced her inner elbow to her wrist. "I'm going to remind you how much you used to love getting high."

"No."

His grin was pure evil. "Oh yes, lovely Jenny. I'm going to strip away the sweet, pure veneer and return you to your true self. A couple of days strung out on my supply, and you'll forget this place exists. You'll be dependent on me again. I'll be the center of your world, just like old times." He slid a strand of her hair between his fingers. "Who knows? Maybe I'll decide to keep you around for a while."

Jade's knees buckled, and she would've sunk to the ground if he wasn't imprisoning her.

Axel obviously hadn't guessed Henry was his child, and she would do anything to keep it that way. Even if it meant leaving Serenity without her son.

Cruz braced a hand on the kitchen sink and stared out the window. He'd heard Jade leave the house and, quickly dressing, had tracked her petite form across the yard.

He decided coffee was necessary to fuel the coming confrontation. His gut churned. She'd duped him. Not only him, but the rest of the team.

The instant York told him their victim was a US marshal, his mind had made the leap to witness protection. Her evasiveness about her past. Her "break" with her family. The utter lack of information about Henry's father. Everything fit.

If he was right, it could mean she was a family member of a person in WITSEC, a witness to a crime or a criminal who turned on a bigger criminal.

Judging by her reaction last night, he was going with criminal. The fear that flashed in her expressive eyes had been mixed with the dread of discovery.

Slamming the mug into the sink, he shook off the hot liquid that splashed on his hand. He was almost to the door when he remembered the sleeping boy. Had his fit of pique awakened him?

Cruz walked lightly around the table and down the hall. He peeked inside the guest room, his chest squeezing at the sight of Henry's face under the halo of white-blond hair. Criminal acts almost always exacted a price from the innocent. What had Jade done to warrant government protection?

He snagged his coat from the hook by the door and put

it on, then shoved his feet into his boots. As he approached the barn, a spontaneous prayer formed in his mind. *Help me keep my temper in check, Lord.*

His stride slowed. He'd had a strong relationship with God as a teenager, buoyed by his parents' faith and a close-knit church youth group. Sal's death had made him question everything, including God's goodness. Even though his faith had wavered, there were times he longed for a renewed intimacy with the Lord, when he knew he couldn't make it on his own strength. This was one of those times.

As he entered, he heard a man's voice. Jade's response communicated her terror. His hackles rose. He hadn't brought his weapon or his phone.

A stranger emerged from Gunsmoke's stall before he had a chance to formulate a plan. Big guy. He outweighed Cruz by at least fifty pounds. His hair was obviously dyed, because it looked unnatural against his pale, freckled skin. His blue eyes locked onto Cruz, and his brows slammed down. He yanked Jade against him and held a long, deadly blade to the underside of her chin.

"Axel, don't." With both hands, she gripped his thick wrist.

This man wasn't a stranger to her. Had she tossed his name to Cruz on purpose?

"I'm unarmed." Cruz lifted his hands in a placating gesture. "Let's make a deal. Leave her, and I'll wait an hour before alerting the police. Plenty of time to get out of town."

"No deal." His upper lip curled, and he dragged her toward the opposite exit. "Jenny and I have unfinished business."

Cruz ground his teeth together. Her real name was Jenny. Confirmation she was living and working in his town under an assumed name. But at that moment, he didn't care what her story was. He was afraid for her. Axel's eyes were soulless.

He slowly advanced. "I can't let you take her."

"You don't have a choice, Officer."

Jade cried out, and blood dripped from her neck.

Cruz's chest rumbled with an utterance that didn't sound human. His fingers furled and unfurled, and he mentally cataloged the items in his tack room in search of a makeshift weapon. He kept his gaze fixed on Jade, silently communicating he wasn't going to abandon her.

Tears streamed down her cheeks. "Let me go," she whispered.

The words weren't directed at her captor. They were meant for him.

He rejected them outright, giving a small shake of his head.

"She gets another slice with each step you take," Axel warned, continuing his retreat.

Jade's eyes were pools of misery. She pressed her lips into a thin line. She didn't protest. Didn't plead for mercy. She was resigned to her fate. Why?

They backed out of the barn and took measured steps, the knife still poised for maximum damage, closer and closer to the woods. Sweat poured off Cruz. The inaction was killing him. Axel shifted his bulk, seized her upper arm and forced her into a run.

Cruz spun on his heel, raced into Gunsmoke's stall and hauled himself onto the horse's bare back. It had been a while since he'd ridden without a saddle. Gunsmoke wasn't thrilled, either, but he obeyed his commands. Axel and Jade had already been swallowed up by the woods. Axel was sure to have a mode of escape stashed in the trees. Cruz had to reach them before it was too late.

Gunsmoke's hooves pounded the earth. Cruz ducked

to avoid getting whacked by low-slung branches. He had to rescue her. For Henry's sake.

He spotted them, surprised at the amount of ground they'd already covered. Axel heard his approach. Glancing over his shoulder, he scowled, his features hardening. Cruz saw the glint of the knife blade. Saw it cut into Jade's side.

Axel shoved her to the ground and fled.

She clutched at the wound and scrambled on her hands and knees toward Cruz. He dismounted and helped her stand.

"Can you ride?"

At her nod, he boosted her onto Gunsmoke and hauled himself up behind her. At the barn, she sagged against the wall, bent over and panting, while Cruz quickly returned the horse to his stall.

Cruz scooped her into his arms and carried her inside the house. The bloodstain on her shirt was growing. He debated where to take her and, in an effort to shield Henry, decided on his own room. He laid her carefully on the bed.

"I need to check the wound."

She didn't acknowledge him. Her eyes were closed, mouth clamped tightly. Against the backdrop of his maroon-and-navy bedding, her skin was nearly translucent, the delicate blue veins visible.

He slid the torn and bloody material up. The slicing wound was right above her waistband.

"It's not deep, nor is it a puncture wound. I can patch it temporarily here."

"All right." Her lips barely moved, and her eyes remained closed.

While fetching the first aid kit, hot water and cloths, he called dispatch first and Mason second. When he returned, he found Jade sobbing into his pillow.

Apprehension slithered through him. Had he misjudged the severity of her injury?

"Jade, talk to me." He crouched by the bed and instinctively held her hand. "I'll take you straight to the hospital if that's what you want. I've got over-the-counter pain reliever—"

"It's not that."

Her tears gutted him. "He's gone, Jade. You're safe. Henry's safe. Police are searching for him now."

Her shoulders quaked with the force of her sorrow. Cruz sat on the mattress and tucked her hand against his chest.

If it wasn't the pain, then what—

He recalled the moment she'd urged him to let her go, and a thought formed in his mind. Henry. She must have thought he would be safer if she left with this Axel person. But why? He hadn't attempted to abduct the boy. The boy...

If this Axel was Henry's father, Jade would do anything to keep him away from him. She'd even be willing to sacrifice her life for the sake of her son.

Her eyes popped open. "Leslie. I need to talk to her. Tessa, too."

"Not now. We have to clean you up before Henry comes looking for you."

Her eyes were red, her nose pink and her lips trembling. "There's a good chance I'm not going to make it through this. I have to be sure someone I know and trust will raise my son after I'm gone."

NINE

Cruz looking startled was new to her. His grip on her hand tightened. His mouth opened. Closed. Then resolve settled over his features, and he was the self-assured police officer once again.

"Our unit is going to protect both of you."

You don't know what I've done. She didn't say the words aloud. Not yet. He would have to be told. If she didn't offer the information, he'd ask questions. That much she knew.

Jade swiped at the moisture on her cheeks. He released her hand to fetch tissues, and she instantly missed the connection.

After disinfecting the cut and applying a bandage, he rummaged in his dresser and returned with a plain shirt the color of magnolia leaves. He hovered by the bed as she sat up, hands waiting to catch her if she swayed. She hadn't counted on the Texan having a nurturing, compassionate side.

"Any light-headedness?"

"No, just feeling weak."

He curled his arm around her upper back and helped her stand, then guided her to the bathroom door. "I'll wait here."

Jade switched out the shirts, amazed at the flimsiness

of her limbs. Her side pulsed with pain, and the nick under her chin smarted. When she opened the door, Cruz arched a brow. The soft cotton shirt engulfed her, hanging almost to her knees. His arm came around her again. As they made their way to the kitchen, she leaned into his side, greedy for the strength and sturdiness he offered. She didn't meet his gaze as she settled into a chair facing the kitchen. He poured a glass of orange juice and placed it in front of her, along with a bottle of pain reliever and a package of oat biscuits.

While she nibbled on the snack, he poured himself coffee and heated water in the microwave. Snagging the single box of tea she'd brought over, he dunked one bag in the mug and brought it to her. He removed his coat, replaced it on the peg and lowered himself into the chair directly opposite her.

"Is Axel Henry's father?"

The reprieve was over. She prayed for courage. She prayed for Cruz's understanding.

"Yes."

"He's the reason you're in witness protection?"

Her stomach flip-flopped. She wasn't surprised he'd guessed the truth, but she hadn't admitted it to anyone outside the USMS. "Yes."

He ran his hand over his hair and kneaded the back of his neck. She waited while he processed the information. "What happened?"

"You mean, what did I do? You're sure you want to know?"

His gaze remained steady, his expression a blank canvas.

"I was attending university in Gainesville, Florida, and living the standard student life when I met Axel at a club. He was attractive. Older. Had a hard edge that intrigued me." The laugh that escaped was harsh and grating. "I was looking for excitement, and he delivered."

"In the form of drugs."

Embarrassment flooded her cheeks. "It started with the cheap stuff and progressed to addictive substances. Soon enough, the drugs dictated my everyday choices. My good grades tanked. I got placed on academic review and kicked off the cheer team. I stole from my roommates. Begged friends for money."

She dug her fingernail into a scratch in the table. Speaking of that time brought the painful, shameful memories to the surface.

"I burned all my bridges until Axel was my only person. A dangerous position to be in, but that's how he liked it."

Axel's threat thrummed through her, making her lungs squeeze until she thought she'd suffocate. Death would be preferable to what he had planned for her.

"I became an addict and a dealer. I chucked any morals I might've had and sold product to anyone with green to spare. I robbed grocery stores, pawnshops, you name it… all to subdue the monster inside me. I stood by while Axel beat his best friend to the point of death, and I couldn't find it in myself to care."

Cruz offered nothing but stoic silence. It was hard to look at him and even harder to stomach the loss of his regard. Although his facial muscles were arranged into a controlled mask, he couldn't hide the anger and disdain in his molten brown eyes. Did he wish he'd let Axel take her?

"I understand this is as difficult for you to hear as it is for me to say. I've heard about your brother."

Beneath the table, his knee bobbed incessantly. He shoved his chair out so fast that she jerked back. He stalked to the island, rested his balled fist on the counter and stared out the window.

"Then you're aware of my hatred for drugs and the havoc they cause."

"I am."

"Sal got sucked into that life thanks to one of his football teammates. He became uninterested in school. Quit his part-time job. I was sixteen at the time and didn't understand what was happening. All I knew was my hero older brother had changed. He went from a likable, outgoing guy with promise to a sullen, sulking shadow. My parents were beside themselves. They didn't know how to help him." Twisting, he speared her with his gaze. "He owed people money and couldn't pay, so they made an example of him. He was only nineteen."

"I'm sorry, Cruz. When you're deep into it, you don't think how your actions affect other people."

He looked away, presenting her with his stone-faced profile.

"I was fortunate," she continued. "The officers who arrested me wanted to net a bigger fish. They offered me a deal—protection in exchange for my cooperation in capturing Axel. That day was a critical turning point."

"Yeah, well, my brother didn't get the chance to turn his life around."

His hurt was a living, breathing thing crowding out the light in the room. He'd be glad to know she was leaving town. It would be easy for him to forget her and her sordid past. She wouldn't forget him, though.

Jade went to him and laid her hand on his arm. His muscle twitched, and she let her fingers slide away. "I appreciate everything you've done for us. I have to ask for one more favor, though. Will you go to the house with us while I pack some of our things? I don't feel comfortable going alone."

His brow furrowed. "You've already been in contact with the marshals?"

"I'm through with the program. Henry and I will be better off on our own."

* * *

Cruz stared at Jade, wishing she'd told him anything else but this. Her past was stained with the scourge of society, the same illegal lifestyle that had cut short his brother's life and broken his parents' hearts. He respected the fact that she hadn't sugarcoated her actions or offered excuses, but he was sorely disappointed.

Still, he had to convince her that leaving without marshal protection was a mistake. A potentially deadly mistake. "Striking out on your own? Not a smart move."

She hiked up her chin. "It's not ideal, but I can't rely on the marshals to protect us. They didn't tell me Axel escaped prison, and the marshal they finally sent to warn me was murdered steps from my door."

The program was voluntary. If she refused protection, they wouldn't force her, especially considering her part of the deal was done. "If you won't accept help from the marshals, at least stay in Serenity," he urged. "You have the full support of SPD. The mounted unit will be your protection network."

"I can't stay. He knows where to find me, and he wants revenge. But if we leave, he'll have to start fresh. We could go anywhere in the country. Somewhere he won't find us again."

Cruz was surprised at how much he disliked the idea. Why did he feel a personal stake in their safety? "Do you know how to cover your tracks? It's not as easy as it used to be. What about money to support yourselves?"

She pulled the cross pendant from beneath the shirt and pressed it between her fingers. "I've been careful. I have savings."

"I don't like it, Jade. Money doesn't last long when you're traveling, staying in motels and eating out. Putting a deposit on an apartment. What happens if your truck breaks down on the side of the road? Or you get sick?"

Her gaze darted toward the guest bedroom.

"Think about what I'm saying, Jade. Axel's obviously good at getting his needs met while evading authorities. He's crossed several states to reach you and is most likely responsible for the marshal's death. Don't you see you'd be safer here where you can be protected?"

Before she could formulate a reply, Officer Bell arrived to take their statements. Henry was still sleeping when he left around eight o'clock. When Cruz voiced concern, Jade checked on him and reassured Cruz he sometimes slept in.

Mason and Tessa pulled in bearing a box of fresh-baked pastries. The women hugged, and Tessa guided Jade into the living room, where they settled close together on the couch. Cruz watched them. Was Jade planning to ask Tessa to raise her son in case she wasn't around to do it?

"You have a strange expression," Mason said. "Care to share what's on your mind?"

Cruz hadn't noticed his sergeant had come to stand beside him. "Let's go outside."

Out on the back deck, he leaned against the house and crossed his arms. The rough bricks leached their cold into his body. "Her name isn't Jade Harris. It's Jenny something. Don't know the surname."

Mason's brows shot up. "I didn't see that one coming." He took a similar position at the opposite railing and waited for him to explain. Cruz relayed what he knew, which didn't feel like a lot.

Mason grunted and scraped his hand along his bearded jaw. He didn't speak for a while, and Cruz knew to wait him out.

"What are her plans?"

"Not WITSEC. She wants to make a run for it. On her own. I'm trying to convince her to stay and let us handle it."

"And?"

"I don't know."

"Tess and I will take them in."

Cruz thought about keeping his mouth shut. Mason's solution would make things easier for him. He wouldn't have day-to-day interaction with Jade. But he couldn't be selfish and put Mason and Tessa to the trouble. Plus, they had Lily to think about.

"Let me take point on this," he said. "She's my neighbor, after all. If they stay here, they'll be close to their belongings, should they need anything. Henry will probably take comfort in that."

"Her past won't be a problem for you?" Mason's voice rang with doubt.

"I'm a professional. I can separate my private feelings from this task. Besides, I noticed something was wrong the other day between you and Tessa. Whatever's going on, you don't need the extra stress."

His sigh was weighted with sadness. "We're hoping to give Lily a sibling, but Tessa's had several miscarriages."

Cruz's arms dropped to his sides. "I'm sorry, brother."

Mason's devotion to his wife and daughter were well-known around town. He and Lily were as thick as thieves, belying the fact he hadn't known about her until she was three years old. Of course, he must be anticipating being with Tessa throughout the whole process and supporting her through pregnancy. For the first time, he'd get to witness the birth of his child and experience everything he'd missed with Lily.

Surprisingly, Cruz's instinct was to offer to pray for them. He knew they prayed for him, because they'd told him so. They asked him to come back to church at least a few times a month.

"All the more reason for them to stay with me. Focus

on your family and provide backup when I need it. Enjoy what's left of the season."

Christmas was eleven days away. Mason and Tessa had family living in Serenity, and they were involved in church programs. Cruz didn't have parties or gatherings to worry about.

"Thank you."

"Also, I probably won't make it in today. Jade will get more rest here than at the stables."

"No problem. We'll handle the patrols without you."

"Any news on Lindsey?"

"Not yet."

Once inside, Mason veered to the island and helped himself to a pastry. Cruz peered into the living room and discovered the women praying. To his right, he heard a creak. He shifted and spotted Henry's towhead in the thin opening. The boy was staring at him.

Cruz beckoned him over, and Henry ran-hopped to his side. "I'm hungry." A loud rumble from his midsection punctuated the claim.

Smiling, Cruz boosted him into his arms. "You'll be happy to hear we have pastries." Setting him on the countertop, he slid the box over and flipped up the lid.

Henry appeared doubtful. "Mommy makes me oatmeal for breakfast. Sometimes a smoothie."

Mason chuckled softly from across the counter. "Cruz doesn't keep that stuff around."

"That's true. I don't often eat breakfast. It's oat biscuits, peanut butter crackers or one of these."

Henry eyed the selection and pointed to a cream cheese Danish.

"Good choice." While Mason tucked it into a napkin and handed it over, Cruz poured milk into a mug.

Cruz was working on his second croissant when the women joined them.

Henry's face lit up. "Look, Mommy!"

Jade's smile was like the sun breaking through rain clouds. "Good morning, sweet boy."

Coming to stand beside Cruz, she ran her hand lightly over Henry's hair. "Did you sleep well?"

He nodded. "Try this."

She sank her teeth into the flaky pastry and made a humming noise. "Very good."

"I didn't want crackers again." His dubious expression made both Mason and Cruz laugh.

He'd have to stock his pantry with more care if his houseguests decided to stay. The prospect of having Jade and her son here was unsettling for various reasons, but he wasn't a rookie cop. He had years of experience under his belt. He could protect them while keeping his personal views out of it.

Her gaze settled on Mason. "Cruz told you everything?"

He nodded. "It doesn't change anything for me. You're important to us, Jade."

Tessa leaned into her husband, and he anchored her there with his arm. The couple presented a united front.

Her revelation didn't change anything for them because they hadn't lost a loved one to the criminal world she'd inhabited. Their family hadn't been destroyed. Their faith hadn't suffered.

Jade turned to regard him with an expectant expression. What did she think he would say? Words failed him, so he put the ball in her court.

"What have you decided to do?"

TEN

Jade grimaced at her reflection in the bathroom mirror. She hadn't brought her hair dryer with her, because she hadn't counted on being gone long. She hadn't counted on a lot of things.

Why is this happening, God? I like Serenity. This is the only home Henry has ever known. Did I not express my gratitude often enough? Did I take my new life for granted?

She yanked the comb through her wet hair until it hung in a straight, damp curtain past her shoulders.

Was she making the right decision to stand her ground? To stay and fight? She was counting on the mounted police to keep them safe. On Officer Cruz Castillo, specifically.

After Mason and Tessa had left, he'd explained why he was taking lead on her case. Everything he'd said made sense, but she had reservations—chiefly her reaction to the man. Nursing an infatuation with him was a ridiculous endeavor, yet her heart surged ahead like a bloodhound tracking a scent.

It had to be loneliness. A yearning for love had started creeping into her days. When Henry was a baby, she hadn't had the energy or brain space to think about the future. Now, she found herself envisioning a special someone to share her dreams, hopes and fears with. A godly man who'd pray and discuss Scriptures with her. A kind, noble-hearted man who'd love Henry as his own. And, yes, a strong, capable man who'd mow the lawn sometimes and kill the really hairy spiders.

That man is not Cruz Castillo. Sure, he was the dreamy cowboy type who spent his days putting his life on the line for others. But she was the last woman he'd be interested in.

Leaving the bathroom, she went to the living room where she'd left Henry watching television and stopped short. Where was he?

"Henry?" Heart hammering, she veered into the kitchen. "Henry, where are you?"

"Downstairs," Cruz's muffled voice called out.

She approached the open door across from his bedroom and descended the carpeted stairs to a bright, open space below. The walls had been painted a neutral caramel and were bare save for a painted wooden American flag. A comfortable sitting area dominated the rectangular room. The couch was obviously a hand-me-down. A pillow and handmade quilt were stacked on one end, telling her Cruz probably stretched out there while watching the flat screen affixed to the wall.

A chair creaked, drawing her attention to the far end, where Cruz sat in a comfy leather rolling chair before a polished walnut desk. Henry was perched on his lap, a well-loved baseball hat dwarfing his head.

"His show ended," Cruz informed her. "He got bored."

This was obviously where he took care of personal business. His laptop was there, along with an organizer stuffed with unopened mail and a book of stamps.

"Mr. Cruz is a good drawer, Mommy. See?" Her son held up a cutout drawing of a goat.

As she got closer, she saw there were multiple cutouts of various animals, as well as a barn. Cruz had gathered markers, computer paper and scissors. She was stunned that he'd made the effort to keep her son entertained. He could've easily brushed him off or tried to distract him with another show.

"Those are quite good."

He shrugged off the compliment. "How are you feeling?"

Her skin itched beneath his gaze. "Better, thank you."

Her side was beginning to ache again. After her shower, she'd applied butterfly bandages and antibiotic ointment and prayed infection wouldn't set in.

"Did you speak with Belinda or David?"

The married couple who operated the Serenity Vet Clinic had expressed concern for Jade. However, Belinda and her husband had to balance their employees' and patients' needs. "While they sympathize with my situation, they can't afford for me to miss work again tomorrow. We're short-staffed as it is, and Belinda needs me to assist with surgeries."

Jade didn't want to jeopardize her job. She had to support herself and Henry.

Cruz frowned.

Henry twisted slightly and laid his hand flat against Cruz's cheek. "Will you draw me another horse? Like Renegade, this time?"

He didn't act bothered by the overfamiliar gesture. "Sure thing, cowboy."

Jade moved closer until the desk pressed into her leg. She was close enough that it would be natural for her to rest her hand on his broad shoulder. Then he could wind his arm around her waist and hold her against his side.

Stop that. "Are we keeping you from anything?"

He considered which marker color to use. "I'm having

groceries delivered before lunch. Until then, I'm a free agent."

Henry tapped one of the myriad photos spread across the desk. "That's Castillo Ranch."

Jade picked it up. "Beautiful property. Do you visit often?"

His fingers worked with efficiency as he sketched out the horse. "Once a year. Twice, if I can manage it. My folks try to come up here sometimes, too."

She inventoried the photos of people who must be his extended family. She zeroed in on an image of Cruz as a young teenager. He was sandwiched between two other boys.

"Is that you with your brothers?"

"Yes."

"Do you ever think about moving back?"

His hand stilled, and his head remained bent. "I like it here. Fresh start, you know?"

"Yes, I do know."

He finally looked at her, his expression inscrutable.

Henry wriggled to get down. Cruz sat back, watching silently as the little boy shuffled several of the cutouts into his hands, carried them over to the couch and began to concoct imaginary conversations.

"You're good with kids," she said.

He'd been the epitome of patience with Henry since the day they'd met. He was the same way with Lily. He'd once sat for an hour with the pair and played Play-Doh.

"My mom and dad are the eldest of their siblings. Thanks to large age gaps, most of my cousins are much younger than me. Our family has a tradition of frequent gatherings, and the task of minding the kids fell to Sal and me." He pressed his lips together, as if regretting mentioning his brother. He returned the marker to its box and leaned closer to whisper, "Does Axel know he's a father?"

She glanced over her shoulder to be sure Henry was engaged with the cutouts and wouldn't overhear. "I didn't learn of the pregnancy until I was in the program."

Using the toe of his boot, he rotated the chair until he was facing her. "Did you undergo drug testing?"

Jade told herself it was a fair question. "I submitted to testing throughout my pregnancy and for a year after his birth. The marshals provided the resources and counseling I needed to get and stay clean. Leslie was key in my success, though. We worked together at a convenience store in Knoxville, where I first settled. She became my mentor, cheerleader and mother figure, all in one. I don't know if I'd be where I am today without her. I freaked out when I discovered I was pregnant. I was alone in a new city. Taking it one day at a time, trying to make the right choices. Suddenly I had a baby on the way who would depend on me for everything." Her throat threatened to close with remembered panic.

Cruz's brows tugged together. "You couldn't contact your folks."

Her shoulders drooped beneath the weight of sadness. "They have no idea they have a grandson. My younger sister would be an amazing aunt."

Jade had scant information about their lives. She'd been warned not to try and learn things through social media or other online sources, because it could be tracked. She'd obeyed, yet Axel had found her anyway.

"Did you have a chance to say goodbye?"

"The marshals advised against it, and I wasn't in a place mentally to argue my side. They probably think I was killed in the car bomb Axel planted."

Cruz shot to his feet. "He blew up your car?"

The sudden movement brought his chest an inch from her nose. She stepped back so she wouldn't have to wrench her neck to see his face.

"I managed to get a copy of his contacts network for the police. I also wore a wire and asked the questions they told me to. After he got arrested, he figured out it was me and tasked one of his associates to get payback."

The veins at his temple pulsed. "How did you avoid the blast?"

"It malfunctioned when a garbage truck smacked into the bumper." Her stomach clenched. "I'm grateful no one was injured in the explosion, and that I wasn't anywhere near it."

He stared down at her, hands on his hips, and she could practically see him puzzling out something.

"He's had you in his grasp three times now. Why didn't he finish you?"

She winced at his bluntness. "He wants to see me suffer first."

She didn't share the details. It was too terrible to think about, much less put into words.

His phone buzzed. Frowning, he checked the screen. "Groceries are here."

"I'll help Henry tidy your desk."

Cruz studied her for a minute more, obviously reluctant to abandon his line of questioning. When he left, her body sagged with relief.

Seated astride Renegade the next morning, Cruz followed the steers' progress around the arena's outer ring. The mounted unit had come early to the neighboring town's fairgrounds complex for training with the Twin Pines farm. The horses were learning to work a herd. It was a different experience for them. He'd grown up on a ranch, of course, but it gave the other officers a chance to work on their horsemanship in new ways. The farm owners, Jacob and Leah, called out instructions.

Outside the covered pavilion, an unrelenting drizzle licked the earth. His cheekbones and ears ached, and his breath came out in a vapor. Cruz couldn't find his usual enjoyment in training, and it had nothing to do with the miserable weather. Jade was miles away in Serenity. Officers Bell and Weiland had promised to do numerous patrols around the vet clinic, but he couldn't help feeling as if he'd abandoned her. Couldn't stop replaying yesterday morning's close call.

Axel hated Jade. He knew she'd helped authorities put him away and had probably spent a lot of his time in lockup planning his revenge. He wanted her to pay...on his terms. Cruz wasn't about to let that happen.

The officers had also promised to keep an eye on Elaine and Franklin's place. Since Franklin was ex-military and worked from home, Cruz didn't have qualms about Elaine continuing to babysit Henry.

Raven and her mount, Thorn, slowed to a halt in front of him. Cruz guided Renegade alongside them and tried to concentrate on the farmers' words. She shot him a sideways glance full of questions he'd eventually have to answer. When they dispersed for lunch, they dismounted and walked the horses to the nearest stock tank.

She removed her helmet and smoothed her braid. "How's it going with Jade and Henry?"

Jade had agreed it was important to share her story with Raven and Silver. Since Cruz had been busy getting his guests settled yesterday, he'd asked Mason to bring them up to speed.

"She's hanging in there." Jade was proof positive that appearances could be deceiving. She had the appearance of a delicate Southern bloom, but she had grit. "Henry hasn't seemed to pick up on any of the tension."

"He's a great kid."

"Agreed." He hadn't turned out that way by accident. Jade was a good mother, plain and simple. Cruz was still having trouble reconciling the responsible, caring person he knew with the ugly picture she'd painted of her younger self.

"Is having them with you going to be problem? Aiden and I will be happy to take them in. You *say* you've gotten over Denise—"

"Why are we talking about my failed marriage? Jade is nothing like my ex-wife."

An adventure seeker, Denise was bold and brash. Together, they'd burned bright and hot, often clashing on issues both big and small. The discord had eventually outweighed the good times. She'd blamed their demise on his absences. He'd blamed it on her unwillingness to fight for their marriage. She was, after all, the one who'd walked away.

Jade was very different. Patient and easygoing, she exuded contentment. Her sweet manner drew others to her.

"She's a lovely woman in all the ways that matter," Raven said, watching him closely. "She's also in a vulnerable position."

"Are you suggesting I'd take advantage of her?"

"No, of course not. But she's going to need a gentle hand and a hefty dose of compassion."

His phone vibrated. Removing it from his uniform pocket, he saw Officer Bell's name and gritted his teeth.

"Bell, what is it? Are Jade and Henry okay?"

"They're fine." Cruz's chest released. "We've had a robbery at Jim's Pawn Shop. Suspect fitting Axel's description ambushed Jim early this morning, tied him up and got away with several rifles, a pistol and ammo."

Cruz dug his fingers into his forehead. Axel had clearly decided to upgrade his weapon collection. "How's Jim?"

"Shaken up. A customer who had an appointment found Jim's car out back but the doors locked. He decided to contact us. Thought Jim might've had a medical emergency."

"Thanks for the heads-up."

"One more thing. The feds and marshals are setting up shop at SPD. We'll have to run our information and movements through them."

Cruz grunted in response. Those agencies didn't play well with others—or each other. The US Marshals would be champing at the bit to get justice for Prescott, whose identity had been confirmed late last night. He wasn't sure how the power play would work itself out, and he didn't care—extra help running Axel to ground was appreciated. He was just glad they were camping out at the police station and not the stables.

Raven lifted her brows expectantly, and he filled her in. "This isn't good," he finished.

"Axel's illegally acquired arsenal or our law enforcement guests?"

"Both."

After they got the horses loaded, they climbed into the truck cab and accessed Axel's information on the laptop.

He slowly scrolled through the records, his gut clenching. "He's a cold one. He's rumored to have killed or given orders to kill over a dozen people. Nothing that can be confirmed, of course."

"He's good at keeping his hands clean."

"He's good at inspiring fear in everyone around him." Why else hadn't the Gainesville PD gotten someone to testify against him in these murder cases?

Raven stared out the rain-splotched window. "Has Jade talked about the time she spent with him?"

"Not much." Granted, he hadn't asked for more. He wasn't sure he wanted to know the details. "We have to find this guy soon, Raven."

Patrol officers had been canvassing neighborhoods, and they'd alerted local businesses to the potential danger. So far, they'd received tips that led nowhere. It was frustrating. Axel had to eat and sleep, and Cruz doubted he had contacts this far north of Florida.

"With people flooding in over the next few days for the car show, that might not be as easy as we'd like."

He groaned. "I forgot about that." Classic car enthusiasts converged on the Smokies several times a year. Great for the economy, but sometimes the crowds created challenges for law enforcement. "Let's get back to Serenity."

He texted Mason and Silver that they were heading out. Mason responded that they'd be leaving in another half hour. The rain became heavier the closer they got to Serenity. He and Raven were soaking wet by the time they got the horses inside the stables.

"I'm going to be late picking up Jade." He consulted his watch, wishing he had time for a hot shower.

"Go on," she said. "I'll see to the horses."

Cruz hurried back into the onslaught. On the way to the clinic, he wondered if they would be called back out tonight to help with accidents. Already there were places of standing water. At least the ground was warm, preventing the roadways from freezing.

In the clinic parking lot, he texted Jade. Five minutes passed without a response. Impatient, he dashed inside, almost colliding with the receptionist at the door.

Gloria held a key ring in her hand. "Oh, Officer Castillo. I was just about to lock up."

"I'm here to pick up Jade."

"She and Belinda went out to the MacGregor farm."

"When did she leave?"

"About two hours ago. They were supposed to have been back by now, but sometimes house calls take longer than expected." She gestured to the door, keys jingling.

"Thanks."

Out in his truck, Cruz tried to reach Jade. It went straight to voice mail. The MacGregor farm was about fifteen miles away and isolated.

He didn't like that she'd left the clinic without protection and hadn't bothered to contact him. More than that, he didn't like that he was beginning to view her as more than a routine case.

ELEVEN

"The trailer's stuck," Belinda announced over the sound of spinning tires. Easing her foot off the gas, she sank against the worn seat. The wipers swooshed across the windshield, sloshing water around without actually clearing the glass.

They'd finished treating Winston MacGregor's mare and had been on their way out when their mobile supply trailer's rear tire had gotten sucked into the muck.

Jade inspected the sky. Gray clouds were stretched out like a dirty blanket, blocking the light. She checked her phone again. Still no reply from Cruz to her texts, which was odd.

The rain turned the MacGregor farm into a bleak, gray landscape, and she couldn't distinguish the shapes in the distance. If Axel did know her location, this would be a prime time to strike.

"Maybe Winston can use his dually to pull us out," Belinda said.

Headlights slashed across her vision, and she recognized the truck turning into the gravel drive. The relief flooding her wasn't specific to the officer behind the wheel. She would've been as happy to see Mason, Silver or Raven.

Liar. You have a personal interest in Cruz.

After entering her new life, she'd determined not to lie to herself. She'd ignored the internal warnings about Axel, had told herself he wasn't that bad. When his actions proved otherwise, she'd told herself she could change him. When she'd gotten in deep, she'd told herself she couldn't survive without him. Without the drugs. All lies.

Belinda sat up straighter. "Is Cruz here on account of you?"

Jade knew she was on rocky ground with her boss, not because of her skills or job performance, but because of the danger surrounding her.

"Probably checking up on me." She strove for nonchalance. He'd stressed the need for her to take it easy at work today and not strain her injury.

He parked his truck beside them and, before she could unbuckle, rounded the hood and wrenched open her door. Water splattered on her jeans, and she shivered.

"You okay?" The hood of his police raincoat had fallen back, and his hair was plastered to his head.

"I sent you multiple texts, but you know how the signal can be up here. You didn't get any of them?"

"No, I didn't." His gaze flicked past her, and he nodded. "Belinda. Looks like you need some assistance. I've got equipment with me. I can get you out."

He shut the door and quickly worked to get them unstuck.

"The most eligible bachelor in Serenity is at your beck and call, it seems," Belinda said, smiling over at Jade. "Are you finally ready to jump into the dating pool?"

She gave the same answer she always gave when asked why she wasn't dating. "Henry's my priority right now. I'll think about romance when he's older."

"Are you telling me you'd turn down an invitation from

him? Cruz Castillo is a responsible, stand-up guy with a good career. He'd be good to you both."

She thought about the smoothie ingredients he'd ordered from the store. When she'd asked about it, he'd said Henry had mentioned she liked to make fruit and spinach smoothies every day. He'd even gotten the ground flax. When she'd tried to pay him, he'd refused. It had been a kind gesture.

And her main reason for not dating was no longer an issue. Her most dearly guarded secret had been exposed.

He will never see you as anything other than a former drug addict.

The thought was harsh and ugly, but she feared it was the truth. The others in the mounted unit knew her better than he did, and they didn't associate her former choices with a personal tragedy.

Cruz yanked open her door again. "Ready?"

She glanced over at Belinda, who wore a knowing smirk. "See you in the morning."

Pulling up the hood of her coat, she snagged her purse and followed him into the downpour. The lower half of her jeans was soaked through by the time she shut herself inside his truck. Mud splattered her yellow rain boots decorated with chickens.

His cologne enveloped her, and she surreptitiously breathed it in. A country song provided a soft, crooning backdrop to the rain pelting the truck roof.

"I'm glad you showed up when you did," she said, holding her hands near the vent blasting hot air. "Saved us from trekking through the rain and muck back to Winston's house."

Grunting, he backed out onto the road and put the gear into Drive. "To Elaine's, right?"

"Yes, please." A call from Belinda came through, and

she glanced into the side mirror to see the clinic truck poised at the gravel drive's edge. The call was brief.

"Belinda's not heading back to town just yet," she told him when she disconnected. "She has a quick stop to make. A friend's cat is recovering from surgery and has ongoing lethargy." When he didn't comment, she said, "How was training?"

"Good."

She got the feeling he was annoyed with her. "I did try to reach you. I would've called if I hadn't gotten busy with Winston's horse."

His knuckles went white on the steering wheel. "I was worried."

Her stomach went into free fall. "I'd be lying if I said I wasn't worried, too. I'm aware of the risks, but I have to pay the rent and feed and clothe my child."

"I know."

"So, how was training?" she repeated, staring him down.

After a beat of silence, he gave her a rundown of what they'd done with the Twin Pines owners and their cattle.

"What do you like about the mounted police?"

He didn't hesitate. "The horses. People react differently to us when we're on horseback. They're curious and much more likely to approach us than if we're in a patrol car. Every day is different, which I like, and most of our time is spent outdoors."

He'd grown up on a ranch, so that made sense. The road wound through heavily wooded areas. He routinely checked the rearview and side mirrors.

"Why did you choose to be a vet tech?"

His interest surprised her. He wasn't the type to make small talk for the sake of filling silence. "I was one of those kids who could've opened a small zoo and charged admission. I had ferrets, iguanas, parrots, rabbits, dogs, cats...you name it."

"All at the same time?" He guffawed. "Did you live in the country?"

"City." She laughed. "We had a sprawling house with more space than we knew what to do with. My parents allowed me to have as many animals as I wanted, as long as I kept them downstairs in the basement and took care of them. Dad grumbled about the upkeep costs, of course. I eventually got a part-time job scooping ice cream because I was afraid he'd change his mind and make me get rid of them. I did eventually have to find homes for them before I moved into the college dorms. Except for Pete. He was an African gray parrot, and my dad found him amusing. I wonder if he's still with them. They can live between forty and sixty years."

An almost overwhelming yearning to see her mom, dad and sister seized her. She'd essentially buried her family the day she entered the witness program, and she continued to grieve what she'd lost.

"Your parents sound nice."

"I guess you're wondering how I messed up so badly. Bottom line... I didn't appreciate how good I had it until I lost everything. I don't let mistakes go to waste, though. My priorities are in order now."

He slowed and drove around a branch blocking the road. "You didn't finish college in Florida, right?"

"I was forced to drop out because I simply stopped going to class. Once I settled in Knoxville with a fresh start handed to me, I realized I wanted a career. I loved animals, and science wasn't a problem for me, so I chose vet tech. I signed up for classes before I learned about Henry. Leslie convinced me not to drop out."

"Couldn't have been easy to juggle raising a child with college courses and a job."

Again, he stole her breath. That sounded suspiciously like empathy. "Some days were brutal. I lost track of how many times I cried myself to sleep." The words slipped out unbidden.

"You're a survivor."

Her head whipped around. At her shocked expression, he lifted a shoulder, the raincoat sounding like paper rustling.

"I don't like what you did, Jade. That world you got yourself involved in stole my brother's future. Every day, drugs destroy lives across this country. But that doesn't mean I can't see how you've turned your life around."

He returned his attention to the road and braked. An orange-and-white A-frame barricade blocked it. His brows clashed. "I suspected flooding would be a problem. The road crew will be out in full force tonight." He turned the truck around and took the road they'd just passed.

Jade's mind was full of what he'd said. It was refreshing to be able to talk about her real life with someone, even if the truth was difficult for them both.

"There's something in the road."

Cruz applied the brakes. The windshield wipers swooshed back and forth, and in between the swipes, she tried to make out what she was seeing.

"Is that a person?"

His face was grim as he killed the engine and unbuckled his seat belt. He pointed to the left side of the road, where the rear end of a sedan was visible between the overgrowth. "Looks like he hydroplaned and hit the tree. Stay here."

He exited the cab, shut the door and approached the man. Crouching next to him, he felt for a pulse.

Jade held her breath, praying he would be all right.

Then a sound she knew too well ripped through the night, and she screamed Cruz's name.

At the sound of a gunshot, Cruz flattened himself against the pavement and whipped out his weapon. He was in serious trouble. No sight of the shooter. Nothing to hide behind. The truck's headlights were acting as a spotlight.

Another bullet whizzed through the rain near his head.

An engine revved, and his truck lurched forward between him and the sedan. Jade threw open the passenger door.

"Get in!"

Staying low, Cruz dragged the victim over and boosted him into the cab. As Jade reached over to assist him, the driver's side window exploded. Her scream mingled with the sound of breaking glass. Cruz pushed her down while simultaneously shielding the victim, who stirred and moaned.

"Jade?" he called.

"I'm okay." Her whisper was barely audible.

Thank You, Lord. The bullet must've exited the open door without hitting him, because he hadn't heard it enter the truck body.

"Start driving."

He jerked the passenger door closed after they were in motion. Sheathing his weapon, he called dispatch and reported the incident.

"Where to?" she asked.

"Walk-in clinic. They can assess if this guy needs ambulance transport." He wasn't going to ask her to drive forty-five minutes to the nearest hospital.

Rain and wind whipped at her hair. In the glow of the dash lights, he could see she had a viselike grip on the wheel.

"I should've checked with the highway department before taking the detour."

"You think Axel set up the roadblock to lure us here?"

"And caused the accident," he surmised. "To make sure we stopped."

The victim was slumped in the seat between them, head lolled toward Jade. He was probably in his early twenties. The wound on his head was the only obvious injury. Cruz knew he shouldn't have moved him. Leaving him on the road in the freezing rain, at the mercy of Axel's plans, hadn't been an option, however.

"He maneuvered us exactly where he wanted us." Cruz wasn't happy. Why couldn't Axel be one of the duller criminals? "How could you have gotten involved with someone like Axel?"

She winced at the bite in his tone. "Don't lay guilt on me. I've accepted God's forgiveness and grace, and it's unproductive to try and pick up old sins again. I'm a new creation in Christ."

His conscience pricked, he fell silent and mulled over her words.

After the clinic took custody of the victim, Cruz and Jade switched places, and he drove to Elaine and Franklin's. They lent him a tarp, and he fashioned a makeshift covering for the window to keep out the elements. Henry's chatter broke the adults' silence during the ride home, not taking a break even when they picked up pizzas for supper. As they neared his house, Cruz noted a pair of vehicles with government plates in his driveway. Jade must have seen them, too, because she gasped.

"What's the matter, Mommy?" Henry strained against his seat belt.

She tossed a tumultuous gaze at Cruz, and he reached

out and grasped her hand without thinking. "I forgot to tell you we have federal agencies in town." He glanced in the rearview mirror. "Henry, how about you and I have a picnic in your bedroom?"

"In my house?" Henry said, confused.

"The room you and your mom are staying in."

"Mommy doesn't let me eat in the bedroom."

Jade clung to Cruz's hand. "This is a special occasion," she said in an overly bright tone. "Just be careful not to get pizza sauce on Cruz's carpet."

"I'll be careful," he vowed.

Cruz parked behind the SUVs, and two men emerged, wearing windbreakers with the words *US Marshals* across the back.

"Who's that?" Henry asked.

"Someone who wants to talk to your mom for a few minutes." Cruz squeezed her cold fingers and turned in the seat. "Henry, I haven't had a chance to put up my tree. It's a miniature version of yours. Will you help me decorate it?"

Henry's big eyes shifted to Cruz, and he grinned. "Yes, sir!"

Cruz squeezed her hand again. "You've got this," he said softly.

The marshals were grim-faced. They'd lost one of their own thanks to this case. No doubt they would strongly encourage her to continue with the program. Would she change her mind and go with them? He acknowledged that if she did, she and Henry would leave a big hole in his life. He'd gotten used to knowing she was next door. He'd gotten used to seeing her smiling face at the stables, unit barbecues and the Black Bear Café.

He didn't want her to leave, and that troubled him. If he committed his heart to someone again—and that was as unlikely as a white Christmas in Texas—he wouldn't, *couldn't* love a woman who was a constant reminder of the biggest tragedy of his life.

TWELVE

Cruz sat on the guest bed and consumed one slice of meat lover's pizza after another. The boxes were stacked on the bedside table, the top one flipped open to the plain cheese Henry had requested. The five-year-old had a seemingly endless supply of energy. He would take a bite and dart back over to the tree that wasn't much taller than him. A plastic container on the floor next to it held an assortment of sparkly ornaments, and the boy delighted in choosing each one and then finding the perfect spot to hang it.

On this return trip, he eyed Cruz's pizza. "Are you going to save Mommy some?"

He nodded and showed him the contents inside the bottom box. "See? I've left her half. Think that's enough?"

Henry took a sip of clear bubbly soda. According to Jade, he wasn't allowed to drink the caffeinated stuff. He glanced at the closed bedroom door. Occasionally, he heard murmurings or the slide of a chair across his kitchen floor, but he couldn't hear what Jade or the marshals were saying.

To distract himself and Henry, he posed the universal question kids heard this time of year. "What do you want for Christmas?"

His green eyes sparkled. "I asked Mommy for a cat. I

want an orange one. They're my favorite. And a gray one and a black one."

Cruz couldn't help but laugh. "Is that so? What did she say?"

"Maybe." He danced back over to the ornament box.

It was odd that a vet tech who loved animals didn't have any of her own. Perhaps she was waiting until Serenity felt like her forever home. Had she lived with her eyes on the rearview mirror, always looking back and never quite letting herself enjoy the present, wondering if her past was going to catch up to her?

A shame some man hadn't come along to be a father to little Henry. Jade juggled all the responsibilities of a single parent—holding down a job, running a household and raising a child—and she did it beautifully without complaint.

"I want race cars, too. A rocket ship and a stuffed Brachiosaurus."

"A what?"

Henry launched into a speech about the different dinosaurs, and Cruz was amazed at the extent of his knowledge. He couldn't verify the information, of course, but Henry sure did sound convincing.

Cruz heard a door close, followed by engines humming to life out front. A minute later Jade swept into the bedroom.

Cruz rose to his feet.

Henry darted over and threw his arms around her legs.

She smiled down into his upturned face. Framing his cheeks with her hands, she said, "I love you to the moon and back, Henry Wade Harris."

"I love you, Mommy Harris."

A soft laugh escaped, and she lifted her gaze to Cruz. "They're gone," she said unnecessarily.

"Are they coming back?"

Complete the survey below and return it today to receive up to 4 FREE BOOKS and FREE GIFTS guaranteed!

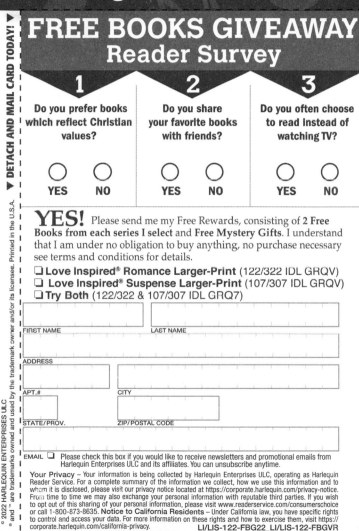

▼ DETACH AND MAIL CARD TODAY! ▼

FREE BOOKS GIVEAWAY
Reader Survey

1

Do you prefer books which reflect Christian values?

◯ YES ◯ NO

2

Do you share your favorite books with friends?

◯ YES ◯ NO

3

Do you often choose to read instead of watching TV?

◯ YES ◯ NO

YES! Please send me my Free Rewards, consisting of **2 Free Books from each series I select** and **Free Mystery Gifts**. I understand that I am under no obligation to buy anything, no purchase necessary see terms and conditions for details.

❏ **Love Inspired® Romance Larger-Print** (122/322 IDL GRQV)
❏ **Love Inspired® Suspense Larger-Print** (107/307 IDL GRQV)
❏ **Try Both** (122/322 & 107/307 IDL GRQ7)

FIRST NAME

LAST NAME

ADDRESS

APT.#

CITY

STATE/PROV.

ZIP/POSTAL CODE

EMAIL ❏ Please check this box if you would like to receive newsletters and promotional emails from Harlequin Enterprises ULC and its affiliates. You can unsubscribe anytime.

Your Privacy – Your information is being collected by Harlequin Enterprises ULC, operating as Harlequin Reader Service. For a complete summary of the information we collect, how we use this information and to whom it is disclosed, please visit our privacy notice located at https://corporate.harlequin.com/privacy-notice. From time to time we may also exchange your personal information with reputable third parties. If you wish to opt out of this sharing of your personal information, please visit www.readerservice.com/consumerschoice or call 1-800-873-8635. **Notice to California Residents** – Under California law, you have specific rights to control and access your data. For more information on these rights and how to exercise them, visit https://corporate.harlequin.com/california-privacy.

LI/LIS-122-FBG22_LI/LIS-122-FBGVR

He held his breath. Would she and Henry be ripped from everything they knew and plunked into an unfamiliar town?

"Not unless I ask them to." A crevice dug between her brows. "I hope I made the right decision."

He didn't dare examine the reasons for the relief sweeping through him.

Henry tugged on her hand. "Come look at the tree."

While she was admiring his work, Cruz pressed a soda and plate piled with generous slices into her hands.

"How hungry do you think I am?"

"As my mama would say, you need to eat to keep up your strength." Taking her shoulders, he turned her toward the bed. "Have a seat while I assist young Henry." Leaning in, he whispered, "That boy of yours is smart as a whip. He just gave me a fifteen-minute lesson on dinosaurs."

Some of the strain receded, and her eyes sparkled with pride. "He surprises me every day with some new tidbit he's learned."

"Is there room in your life for someone special?"

Her jaw sagged.

He held up his hands, ears burning. "I was just thinking you seem to be as gun-shy about relationships as I am. Surely you get lonely."

Instead of answering, she sank onto the bed and stuffed pizza into her mouth.

"Sorry. I was out of line. I certainly don't like when people ask why I haven't found a wife and settled down yet."

She washed down the bite with soda. "I couldn't bring myself to enter a relationship based on a lie."

He sat on the bed beside her and thought about that. The admission told him a lot about her character. Maybe that was why he felt comfortable to share some of his truths. "My first wife left me. Didn't even make it a year."

She didn't act surprised. He'd kept his past close to the vest and initially only told Raven. Eventually, he'd shared it with Mason and Silver.

"Tessa told you?" he guessed.

"She didn't have much to say on the subject."

"That's because I didn't share details in the first place." He studied her. "You were talking about me with Tessa, huh?"

He watched the flush spreading across her face with fascination.

She stuffed another bite into her mouth, and he chuckled. They turned their attention to Henry, who had become absorbed with his task.

"You don't plan to try again?" she said, wiping her mouth with a paper napkin.

He thought how easy it was having her and Henry in his home. He'd been apprehensive at first, but they'd filled the place with conversation and energy he didn't realize he'd been missing.

"I want kids," he admitted without thought.

"But you're not sure you want to risk trusting someone and having them walk away like your first wife."

"Something like that."

"How old were you?"

"Twenty-four when we got married, but we dated for several years before that."

"You're thirty-two now, right? You're surely a different man than you were back then. You've learned, stretched and matured. You won't make the same mistakes you did before."

He searched her face. Jade's outward beauty reflected her heart. She was kind, gentle and loving. Grounded and mature, something his ex-wife hadn't been.

Jade was taking advantage of his inspection to do one of

her own. He saw her gaze lock onto his mouth, saw the interest stir to life in the mossy depths. His heart reared, then galloped against his rib cage. Shock shuddered through him. Was she attracted to him?

Excitement rushed through his veins, and he struggled to rein it in. He'd promised Mason and the others he could separate his personal feelings from his professional duty. That included foolhardy impulses—like wanting to kiss Jade Harris.

Belinda sat behind the desk and her husband, David, lounged beside the dry-erase board posted with surgery dates and patient names. They shared expressions of consternation.

Gloria had pounced on Jade the minute she stepped foot in the clinic and informed her the bosses wanted to see her in Belinda's office. Her stomach was tighter than a drum. She felt hot and flushed.

"We heard what happened last night," Belinda began, leaning forward and folding her hands on the desk. "I'm glad you're okay."

"I am. Okay, that is." She rubbed her damp palms over her scrub pants. "I'm fully capable of performing my duties." Granted, her knife wound was still healing and prevented her from lifting large animals onto the operating table or carrying heavy stuff like pet food or litter bags. But reminding them of her stabbing wouldn't help her case.

David cleared his throat. "The thing is, Jade, we have a responsibility to our patients and their owners. We understand none of this is your fault, but we can't put them or our other employees at risk."

"You're firing me?"

Belinda shook her head. "No, no. You're a valuable employee, Jade. We don't want to lose you. However, we've hired a temporary replacement until your troubles are over. She's coming from middle Tennessee and will be here Monday. You can work the remainder of the week."

Jade stared at the shiny tile floor and pressed her hand to her mouth. What now? How would she pay her rent? Buy groceries? She had savings, but it wouldn't carry them for long.

David pulled an envelope from his pocket, looking both discomfited and sympathetic. "Here's your Christmas bonus."

She accepted the envelope but didn't open it. Usually, they received their bonus on Christmas Eve. "Thank you."

Barking erupted in the reception area. Patients were waiting.

Belinda stood, her chair creaking. "I'm sorry, Jade. Hopefully this situation will be resolved soon."

"Sure." She exited the office and retreated to the break room, where she absentmindedly poured Gloria's strong-as-nails coffee and drank without thinking of the caffeine.

Jade made it through back-to-back appointments, performing her tasks with the constant refrain buzzing in the back of her mind. *No job.* Not even a visit from her favorite standard poodle could dissipate the cloud of anxiety. By lunchtime, she was a mess. She buttoned up her coat and carried her insulated bag to the large enclosure at the rear of the clinic. At this time of year, only the indoor kennels were in use. Grateful for the solitude and quiet, she sat at the picnic table and ate her soup.

What am I supposed to do, Lord? My life is unraveling.

Hard to believe less than a week ago, she'd been reveling in the holiday whirl, anticipating her Sunday school party and trying to decide what to cook for Leslie's Christmas Day gathering. Henry had a role as a sheep in the church play, and she had yet to purchase gifts for Tessa and Elaine. Those things seemed trivial now.

But without faith, it is impossible to please Him. The verse was one of the first Leslie had encouraged her to memorize. "When problems arise, cling to that verse," Leslie had said. Jade had repeated it to herself during those early days of her pregnancy when she'd been overwhelmed with uncertainty and tempted to withdraw from her classes.

I know You love me, Father. I know You're in control. Help me to remember that, no matter what happens.

The rest of the day was easier, although her heart was sad. She told herself she'd get her job back when this was all over, but there was always the possibility Belinda and David would prefer her replacement and decide not to bring Jade back. By the time she sat in Cruz's truck at the end of the shift, her emotions were all over the place.

He let the truck idle and turned off the radio. "What's wrong?"

She wrapped her hand around her cross pendant. "I've been placed on a leave of absence starting Monday," she choked out.

A heavy sigh left him. His hand came to rest on her shoulder. "I'm sorry."

"I don't blame them. They have to do what's best for the clinic. I wouldn't dream of putting others at risk, of course."

She felt bad enough about that young car accident victim. He'd been treated and released with minor injuries, but his car had been totaled. She'd purchase him a new one if she had the money.

"You're not in this alone."

She finally braved a glance in his direction and was stunned to see the depth of his concern. Unable to voice her gratitude without risking tears spilling over, she merely nodded.

As he backed out of the space, she belatedly noticed the tarp was gone. He must've gotten the window fixed on his lunch break.

"I got a call from Detective York during my drive over. They located Axel's hideout. Law enforcement has received a number of tips in recent days, but this one actually paid off. They're searching for clues and trying to establish his pattern of movements. Want to ride along?"

She texted Tessa, who responded that she was happy to let Henry stay longer.

As they drove through town, they shared tidbits about their days. Everything about Cruz intrigued her. He was no longer a distant individual on the fringes of her life. He was becoming a friend. Someone she counted on and trusted. Did he consider her a friend, too? Or was her past too much of an obstacle?

Leaving the center of town behind, they drove down roads flanked mostly by farms. He eventually turned down a wooded street with identical cabins.

"These look like vacation rentals," she said.

"This street connects to a residential neighborhood up ahead."

They progressed through a series of stop signs, passing older homes on postage-stamp lots. On the last street, the yards were bigger and the homes neglected. A few were almost buried beneath a blanket of brown kudzu. Police cruisers and unmarked vehicles were parked on either side of the street in front of a drab gray house with black shutters. Local officers and federal agents milled about.

"Why did he pick this one?" she mused aloud.

"Either the owners aren't around, or he coerced them to help him."

They exited the vehicle, and Jade eyed the candy-colored sky. The pink and yellow splashes would soon be absorbed by darkness.

Detective York met them in the driveway.

"Good news. We intercepted the owner a few minutes ago and are interrogating him inside. Name's Nick Turner. He's been busted twice for possession of marijuana. He'll crack like an egg, I'm sure of it." He gestured to the house. "There's something I'd like to show you."

At the mention of Turner's crimes, Cruz's face hardened to marble. Jade could practically feel his distaste heating the air around him.

The house was sparsely furnished, and little light filtered through the dirty windows. The floors hadn't seen a broom or mop in some time. Jade could hear men conversing in another part of the house. Detective York led them down the hallway to a large bedroom. A mattress was on the floor, along with a table and one camp chair. Chinese takeout boxes and bags containing ramen noodles and tuna cans littered the room.

York picked up a folder from the bed and dropped it on the table, tapping the sleek cover with one finger. "Our man is thorough, to say the least."

Cruz opened it. He stared down at the contents without moving. Jade's feet reluctantly brought her to his side. Photos of her. Dozens of them.

She spread them out with shaking fingers. They depicted her at various times and on different days. Dropping Henry off at Elaine's. Leaving the clinic after a shift. In the grocery store parking lot, loading bags into her truck. Talking with friends on the church steps.

She didn't realize she was close to passing out until Cruz gently pressed her into the chair and curved his broad hand on the back of her neck.

"Put your head between your knees and breathe," he instructed softly, standing behind the chair.

His fingertips gingerly brushed her hair to one side, strand after strand after strand. His other hand came to rest on her shoulder. She closed her eyes and focused on the reassuring contact.

Axel wasn't here, but he had been. He'd stalked her. Taken the time to have the photos printed so he could study her and imagine ways to exact his revenge.

Footsteps clipped along the hall. "Sir? We're done with Turner."

"Thanks, Bell."

Jade slowly sat up, thankful the dancing black dots had disappeared from her vision. Cruz moved to stand beside her, his dark eyes soft and inviting. "You okay?"

She thought fleetingly that she could get used to him looking at her like this. Like he cared. "I'm good."

"What did you find out, Bell?" York asked.

Officer Bell's gaze touched on Jade before returning to his notepad. "Axel broke into the home about ten days ago. He issued an ultimatum. Either Turner helped him, or he'd kill him. He's rattled."

"When did he see Axel last?" Cruz asked.

"This morning. He doesn't know where he went. Axel didn't keep him apprised of his comings and goings. Sometimes he'd task Turner with getting food or other supplies." He lifted his gaze. "Oh, the blue and white motorcycle you saw at Franklin and Elaine Latimer's place is registered to Turner and is parked in the shed."

"What's Axel driving now?" York asked.

"Turner doesn't know."

"Or he claims not to know," Cruz muttered.

"We've collected all the guns Axel stole from the pawnshop except for a semiautomatic rifle and a handgun. Also, several boxes of ammo."

Bell returned to the other part of the house, and York walked around until he was facing them. His eyes rested on her. "Ms. Harris, is there anything you can tell me that will aid this investigation?"

"Nothing that you don't already know. Axel doesn't care who he hurts as long as he gets what he wants."

York nodded. "The reports are in from CSU. We were able to positively link evidence at the murder scene to Axel. He's responsible for the murder of US Marshal Prescott."

Jade could only nod in acknowledgment. An innocent man's blood was on her hands. Fear chewed up her insides and spit them out. What if Cruz met the same end?

Cruz's brows tugged together. "What exactly did Axel say to you in the barn that morning? There could be some detail we overlooked."

She bit her lip. Both men stared at her, waiting.

"He plans to get me hooked on drugs again."

Fury surged in his eyes. He visibly fought to control his reaction, his fingers clenching and unclenching. When he spoke, his words were underscored with icy resolve.

"I refuse to let that happen."

Jade wanted to believe that. The alternative was too terrible to contemplate.

THIRTEEN

Cruz had encountered all sorts of criminals during his career. On a scale from annoying to evil, Axel dipped toward the worst of the worst. He *enjoyed* other people's misery. He'd watched Jade for days and had seen how she'd turned her life around. The best way to exact his revenge was to rip away her freedom and reduce her to the dependent addict she used to be.

His stomach churned.

Axel had lost his hideout and errand boy, but he'd proved he was resilient. He'd find a way to meet his needs.

The piano at the other end of the fellowship hall abruptly stopped, halting his thoughts. The children's voices that had filled the hall for the past hour faded uncertainly. Mason's sister, Candace, was the choir leader, and she gave them instructions in a singsong voice. Sandwiched between Lily and Kai, Henry stood on the second row of the makeshift bleachers, his blond hair shining beneath the bay lights overhead.

The airy room was abuzz with activity as volunteers pitched in to help prepare for the upcoming Christmas pageant. This was the last place he'd expected to come tonight. As they were leaving the Turner residence, Jade had informed him that Henry had practice. His first instinct was to argue against it, but she'd explained that he'd been practicing for months, learning the songs and accompanying hand motions, and he would be devastated if he didn't get to participate. So Cruz had gotten on the phone and asked some buddies from patrol if they'd stand watch outside the church for a few hours. Mason would be there, as well.

Cruz had planned to remain on the perimeter and keep watch. Instead, he'd been roped into painting sets with the other parents. He and Jade were working on a storefront. They were in the farthest corner from the choir, in a dead zone of activity. He was painting a faux-brick exterior. She was painting windows, adding realistic details like frost, sparkle, garlands and ornaments. She worked with painstaking care, as if this was going in an art gallery.

He put his paintbrush in the can and arched his stiff back. "You're good at this."

A becoming blush splashed across her cheeks, and he surmised she wasn't used to getting compliments.

"I did set design for the high school drama club. My favorite production was *Beauty and the Beast*. The backdrops were ornate. The schedule was demanding, but I loved every minute."

"Why didn't you pursue art as a career? Or theater?"

"I considered it. My parents convinced me to consider other options. I entered as an undecided major and never did narrow it down." She contemplated her work and leaned in to add swipes of silver to the ornaments. "I was involved in the university theater department my freshman and sophomore years, but I stopped when I had to choose between that and volleyball."

"Did you play in high school?"

"Yes. We were a tight-knit group."

"Artistic and sporty," he drawled. "Were you voted most popular, too?"

Her green eyes flashed in surprise, and she laughed, a husky, pleasant sound that warmed him. "Not quite."

He didn't have any trouble picturing her as a teenager. She had probably been one of those students who didn't belong to any one group, someone who was friendly to everyone, regardless of social standing.

"Someone as beautiful and kind as you must've had your fair share of admirers."

Her lips curved sweetly. He was tempted to reach out and skim his thumb over them. Test their softness. Lean in and—

"I had a steady boyfriend my senior year."

Shocked by his thoughts, he forced his gaze to roam the room. "Let me guess—the star quarterback."

"Point guard. He accepted a basketball scholarship in a different state, and we decided against the long-distance thing. I didn't date again until Axel. If I'd been in a relationship, I wouldn't have noticed him that night. But then, I wouldn't have Henry."

The hitch in her voice brought his focus back to her. He longed to make things right for her. He even wanted her to experience a sincere, loving relationship with a stand-up guy.

She gestured to his half-finished brick wall. "You're not so bad at this yourself. Were you in drama club, too?"

"Me? No way. Ranch operations dominated my after-school hours."

"You weren't involved in sports? I pictured you as a football player."

"That was Sal. He made it clear ranching wasn't in his future. He was hoping for a football scholarship as his ticket out of Texas."

"Did your other brother play?"

"Diego? Nah, he was like me. More interested in being

with the horses. My parents wouldn't have let us play even if we'd expressed interest. Sal got introduced to drugs by some teammates, and they were petrified of losing another son to that life."

"What are your parents like?"

"They're firm believers in hard work. God and family are their foundations. Mom and Dad grew up on neighboring ranches. Their parents were friends and occasionally had dinner together. Dad likes to say he fell in love with her *sopapillas* before falling in love with her."

"Ah, the girl next door," she teased. She stopped and ducked her head, blushing again.

Was she thinking that she was *his* girl next door? He shook his head, stunned he'd go there.

"Will you spend Christmas with them?"

"I typically go to Texas after Christmas. We have a late celebration, and I stay through New Year's. What about you?"

"Henry and I go to the church's Christmas Eve candle-light service and spend Christmas Day with Leslie and her family. They've basically adopted us at this point."

He'd seen them at the candlelight services before he'd stopped going. "What were your holidays like growing up?"

"My mother was big on volunteering, so we served at various organizations throughout the year. The weeks leading up to Christmas were busier. We wrapped presents for charities, helped at soup kitchens and delivered food dona-tions to shut-ins. My parents, sister and I exchanged gifts on Christmas Eve because we had several stops to make on the twenty-fifth. Two sets of grandparents, as well as an elderly aunt and uncle."

"Sounds hectic."

"It was a whirlwind, for sure. I might've complained a

time or two." Her smile didn't last. "I know what I'm missing now. I'd give anything to hug my grandma Hazel. She and I were especially close."

"Do you know how she's doing?"

Her expression was pained. "If she's alive, she just celebrated her eighty-first birthday."

"Now that Axel knows your location, there's nothing stopping you from contacting your family."

It was obvious she'd contemplated it. "I'm scared to reach out. Will my parents want a relationship with me? Will they reject Henry because of who his father is? I don't know what to do. The decision will have to wait. Either Axel will be captured, or..." She trailed off, probably picturing in her mind's eye the other scenarios. "Or he won't."

Without thinking, he slid his hand beneath the silken curtain of her hair and cupped her cheek. Her eyes were sad and troubled, and he wished he could promise everything would be okay. "No matter what happens, you can count on me. I won't leave your side."

She turned her face into his palm, reaching up to hold his hand in place. His nerve endings fired, jolting him. "I don't know how I'll ever repay you."

His mind emptied of all thoughts but one—he was not immune to Jade Harris, after all.

The noise around her faded to a low hum. Cruz's espresso eyes invited her closer. His mouth, which could be so stern and forbidding, was soft and relaxed. She could see the proof in his face—he felt the same pull as she did. If they were alone, she felt sure this moment would mark a turning point. But was that wise? For either of them?

"Cruz. Jade." Mason's voice snapped the connection. They dropped their hands simultaneously. She turned to face Mason and Tessa.

Mason's gaze was sharp, watchful. Tessa, on the other hand, looked like a cat with a bowl of cream.

Cruz's face was angled away, so it was hard for her to gauge his thoughts.

"Mason decided it was time for punch and cookies. Want to join us?" Tessa gestured to the snack table in the opposite corner. Several people had congregated there to chat.

"I could use something to drink," she said, getting to her feet.

"I'll pass," Cruz said.

Mason crossed his arms. "Tessa, can you bring me some?"

"Sure." She linked her arm with Jade's as they walked away. "I have a feeling Mason's going to grill Cruz."

"Why would he do that?"

Tessa's hazel eyes veered to her, laughter in them. "You aren't aware of how cozy you two looked just now. In fact, I'm sure you forgot where you were for a while."

Jade glanced over her shoulder. Cruz was standing, arms folded across his chest, mirroring Mason's stance. Their conversation was obviously a serious one.

"He was merely reassuring me." She attempted to dismiss the emotionally charged moment.

At the table, Tessa poured them each a cup of bright green punch. "I'm not buying that. You like him, don't you?"

She sipped the chilled lime-flavored drink and grimaced. "Liking him would be a very bad idea."

"He's a great guy. He has deeply held convictions and a strong thirst for justice. His intensity intimidates some people. Is that what has you worried?"

"Didn't even cross my mind. I admire his passion."

"Then what is it?"

"He's a cop. My past disqualifies me."

Tessa touched her arm. "Forget your past. It's what you do with your present that matters."

She knew that, but she wasn't sure Cruz saw it that way.

"Your ex's return has likely stirred up memories of a bad time, but don't forget who you are now. Whose you are."

After years of searching for peace in all the wrong places, she had found meaning and belonging in Christ. She was loved and forgiven.

"Cruz hasn't shown an inkling of interest in a woman since he moved here," Tessa continued. "But he's different around you."

Jade ignored the hopeful leap of her heart. She had to be responsible. She had to do what was best for Henry. For Cruz, too. He'd been hurt and abandoned by his ex-wife. His next relationship should be with someone who didn't come with baggage.

Candace released the kids, and they streamed through the room. Lily and Henry were already with Mason and Cruz by the time she and Tessa reached them. Tessa handed Mason a napkin full of cookies, which he proceeded to share with the kids.

Cruz met Jade's searching gaze and gave her a tight smile.

"Is Lily coming to my birthday party?" Henry spoke around a mouthful of cookie.

Jade frowned. She'd forgotten about her own son's party. She'd scheduled it months ago and sent invitations to ten kids. The arcade was an overwhelming experience on a good day. During the holiday break, when the weather outside pushed the kids indoors to cure their boredom, it was over-the-top. Certainly a security nightmare. Too much activity and noise and places to hide.

"Of course Lily is invited."

Henry and Lily hopped around the group of adults, whooping and laughing. Kai and others joined in.

Jade looked between Mason and Tessa. "I have to cancel the party."

She'd felt guilty enough asking Cruz and the other officers to babysit them for this final practice and the upcoming performance. She couldn't expect them to put their life on hold every time she had an event on her calendar.

"Where's it supposed to be?" Cruz asked.

"The arcade."

His forehead furrowed. "That would be tough to contain."

"Maybe you should tell him you're going to postpone the party instead of outright canceling it," Tessa suggested.

Henry was going to be upset, either way.

"Let me give it some thought before you decide," Cruz said.

Tessa corralled the kids so that Cruz and Jade could finish their project. Mason was enlisted to help carry the wet set pieces into the hallway to dry.

After they'd been painting in silence for some time, Jade stopped and watched him work. He must've sensed her attention, because he sat up and raised his brows.

"Something on your mind?"

"Is everything okay between you and Mason?"

He thought about his response. "The line between personal and professional gets blurred sometimes."

She parted her lips to ask for specifics.

He held her off. "We're okay. Our unit functions like a family. We have differences of opinion, snipe and squabble, but we always make up in the end."

She'd been around the officers long enough to know he spoke the truth. "I don't like being the cause of discord, though."

"Please, don't worry about it."

The word *please* didn't come out of Cruz Castillo's mouth often, which made her sit up and pay attention. "I'll try not to."

"I guess that will have to satisfy me." He winked, his mouth curving in a toe-curling smile.

She returned to her painting, although there was a slight quiver in her fingers. They finished almost an hour later and carried the pieces to the hallway. By that time, Henry's energy was flagging. Mason accompanied them to Cruz's truck, his mood solemn. She appreciated that he cared about her welfare, but she truly didn't want to cause trouble. Before she could think of something to reassure him, Officer Weiland drove up and said there wasn't anything unusual to report. Weiland followed them home, waiting at the end of the driveway as they exited the vehicle.

Henry had fallen asleep in his car seat. Without a word, Cruz unbuckled him and hoisted him into his arms. He handed her the house keys and, as soon as they were through the door, waved to Weiland and pivoted inside to disarm the security system.

He'd left the end table lamps on in the living room, as well as the hood light above the stove. The white wall tiles and the farmhouse sink gleamed in the semidarkness. The heater kicked on, chasing away the chill they'd carried inside. His extra coat hung on a peg beside the door, and she smelled his cologne each time she walked past it. His home was becoming familiar. Comfortable. A welcoming haven of rest and security.

Cruz carried Henry into the guest room, laid him gently on the bed and removed his shoes. Henry stirred and mumbled something about peanut butter crackers.

Cruz aimed a quizzical smile at Jade. "How can he have room after all those cookies?"

"Anything to postpone bedtime," she murmured, removing clean pajamas from the dresser drawer. "Come on, Henry, let's go to the bathroom and brush your teeth."

To her surprise, Cruz was still in the room when they returned.

He tousled Henry's hair, his face softening with fondness. "Sweet dreams, cowboy."

Henry snuggled beneath the covers. "Will you read to me, Cruz?"

"It's late. Maybe tomorrow night."

"Will you pray with me?"

Cruz hesitated a moment before kneeling beside the bed. Jade's heart skipped a beat. Once Henry had Cruz's hand in his grip, he turned his big eyes toward her and extended his other hand. "Mommy, it's time to pray."

She scooted onto the bed on his other side and sandwiched his hand between hers. Her gaze locked with Cruz's, and she felt something shift inside her. He bowed his head and began to haltingly beseech God for His protection and mercy. As the prayer continued, his voice became stronger and filled with conviction—proof Cruz hadn't walked away from his faith forever.

Longing consumed her. What woman wouldn't want a dreamy, honorable cowboy cop as her own? A man who fought for justice and protected the innocent and vulnerable? A man who loved Jesus as much as she did?

Longing for something with all her heart didn't make it achievable. This feeling that she, Henry and Cruz were a family was deceptive, a lie she could easily let herself believe. A dangerous lie for them all.

FOURTEEN

Cruz and Silver walked out of the stables together at shift's end the next day.

"You heading to the clinic?" Silver asked, pulling the collar of his black jacket up when a stiff wind blew through the parking lot. The building lights lit up the entire space, as well as part of the paddock.

"It's gonna be a long night." Jade had called him an hour ago and said the night-shift vet tech had called in sick, leaving her to fill the slot. Animals recovering from surgery needed round-the-clock care. Henry would sleep at Mason and Tessa's.

He was relieved Jade wouldn't be at the clinic after this week. While he understood her concerns about lost wages, he couldn't help feeling uneasy when they were apart.

"I considered picking up her favorite meal from the Black Bear, but she's been alone for half an hour at least. I'll have something delivered instead."

"You know her favorite meal? This is getting serious."

"Don't start."

"What's her favorite color? Espresso, like your eyes?" Silver grinned and waggled his brows.

Cruz rolled his eyes. Inwardly, he wondered about the answer to that question. The more he learned about Jade, the more he wanted to know. Silver couldn't discover that, however. He'd be relentless.

"Jade and I are too preoccupied with her ex-boyfriend to worry about individual preferences. We just so happen to have eaten several meals together. That's the only reason I know she orders the strawberry spinach salad every time. She's a healthy eater." His mom would like that.

Silver cocked his head to the side. "You like her."

"Don't you have somewhere to be? Like with your wife?"

"You don't deny it, then." Triumph gleamed in his eyes. "Lindsey thinks you two are perfect for each other, you know."

He grunted. "How is Lindsey?"

"Trying to distract me, huh?"

They reached their trucks, parked side by side, and Cruz hit the unlock fob on his key ring. His truck lights flickered in response.

"She hasn't fainted again. Around the holidays, she gets busy and forgets to eat. She's taken a larger role in the Christmas with Cops children's program this year, on top of everything else." He opened his truck door and tossed in his duffel bag. "I text her throughout the day and ask if she's eating. I've become a nag."

Silver had changed. He no longer tried to hide his scars or pretend his past hadn't happened. He was less guarded. He smiled more. Joked more. He was happier. Because of Lindsey.

Cruz thought about how Jade and Henry had changed his life in such a short time. Last night, when Henry had asked him to pray, Cruz had been knocked for a loop. The boy's innocent request had humbled him. And as he'd prayed, he realized the futility of holding on to bitterness and anger. He was only hurting himself. Plus, he'd really missed being close to God.

He'd gone to his own room, pulled out his Bible and had a long talk with the Lord. He'd asked for forgiveness and help healing his stubborn heart.

"Another fault to add to your already lengthy list," Cruz quipped. "I don't know how she puts up with you."

"Because I'm lovable and handsome, that's why."

"See you tomorrow."

Their work schedules weren't always Monday through Friday. Occasionally, they had an event or training on the weekends. Tomorrow, they would complete drone training. Jade had promised him use of a cot for tonight, but he didn't plan to sleep. His job was to watch over her while she watched over the animals in her care.

When he pulled into the clinic lot, he surveyed the property and its surroundings. He didn't particularly like what he saw. The clinic was located on a lonely stretch of road, out past the underground caverns tourist site, and backed up to woods. A car mechanic business was across the street. The building had been neglected, and the signage for Bob's Garage had all but succumbed to time and weather. There were cars in the closed bays, however, and the tall privacy fence bordering the adjacent lot looked relatively new.

He texted Jade and climbed out of the truck, duffel bag in hand. She met him at the door, her petite frame outlined by golden light deeper in the building.

Her smile was shy, sweet and only for him. He entered, unable to keep from brushing against her as they traded places in the hallway. Beneath the smell of dog hair, pet food and disinfectant, he detected her flowery shampoo. She turned the lock and tested the handle.

Her Christmas scrubs matched her eyes. When she'd

climbed into his truck this morning, her unbound hair had gleamed like strands of moonlight. She'd pulled it into a makeshift knot at some point during the day.

"I didn't think to ask if you had pet allergies."

He shook his head. "But I am allergic to Valentine's Day, erratic drivers and fancy coffee concoctions."

As they passed the exam rooms, she tilted her head in his direction. "I don't drink coffee often, as you know, and I agree with you that bad drivers should stay home. But what's wrong with Valentine's Day? You don't like stuffed bears and chocolate truffles?"

"Forced expressions of love? Inflated flower prices? High expectations no man can meet? No."

She chuckled. "Don't hold back."

He rubbed the back of his neck. "My ex-wife was picky," he confessed. "Any gift I brought home—whether for Valentine's, birthday or just because—wasn't good enough. I guess that's tainted my view."

Her sneakers squeaked against the tile as she led him into a room that was the hub of the clinic. Christmas lights were strung around the doors, flashing in patterns of vivid colors.

"For me, it's not the gift that matters," she said. "I appreciate when someone takes the time to pick out something special. That they thought about me, you know?"

Of course, Jade would have that outlook. He thought about what she'd said before. "Chocolate truffles, huh? I thought you didn't do dessert."

"I do healthy versions of dessert," she corrected, smiling. "I do have one weakness—dark chocolate and orange. That's a combination I can't resist."

He filed the information away along with other tidbits he'd collected about her during this week of close contact. For what purpose? As soon as Axel was in handcuffs, their obligatory connection would be severed. They'd return to normal life. He'd be busy with his work and his antidrug campaign, and she'd continue raising her son and caring for Serenity's animals.

She opened a door in the corner. "This is Belinda's office. I've already set up the cot. You can put your duffel in here."

A cat's pitiful mewling caused her to frown. He counted ten kennels built into the wall on their right.

"Excuse me for a second."

After stowing his duffel on the floor beside the desk, he took a moment to familiarize himself with the T-shaped building. The front section housed the lobby and reception desk, as well as the exam rooms. This back section held two offices—one for Belinda and one for her husband— a large supply room, a closet-size break room and an operating room.

A stainless steel table dominated the middle of the space. Glass-fronted cabinets lined the wall opposite the kennels.

There were three exits. The main one, a second between the exam rooms and bathroom, and a rear one leading to an enclosed kennel area. There wasn't an alarm system, which bothered him.

Jade held an orange cat tucked against her chest. The cat's eyes were droopy and bloodshot and appeared to be smeared with a clear, goopy substance. He'd stopped crying the moment she picked him up. Smart cat.

Cruz went closer. "What's he in for?"

Her nose scrunched. "You make it sound like he's in jail."

"He is. Vet jail."

"Pumpkin snuck out of his owners' house and got attacked by a stray dog. We were able to save his leg, but he has to stay here for observation for a couple of days."

"Poor fella." He reached out his hand. "Can I?"

"Sure."

He let the cat sniff his fingers before stroking the downy fur.

"Don't worry," she cooed softly to the feline. "Cruz may look big and scary, but he knows how to be gentle."

Cruz realized he'd spent more time alone with Jade than he had with any woman since moving to Serenity. He liked being around her.

Lowering his hand, he drifted to the cages and peered in the occupied ones that didn't have blankets covering the doors.

"Why does this beagle have photos taped up in there?" he asked softly. The dog's eyes were open, but she didn't lift her head.

"Sadie is recovering from pneumonia, and she's anxious without her family." She came to stand beside him. "Her mom and dad provided the pictures and that chew toy, which is her favorite. Believe it or not, things from home calm them."

"How many overnighters do you usually have?"

She shrugged. "As you can see, we're not equipped to handle a lot of patients. Tonight we have six. Most of these patients are here because they had a scheduled surgery. We refer emergencies to the larger clinic in Maryville."

"You love what you do, don't you?"

"I do. Sometimes it gets stressful, like any other job, but I like that each day is different." She cuddled the snoozing cat closer and kissed his head. "It's rewarding when we help them feel better and in turn make their humans happy."

"I feel the same about my work. There are challenges,

and some days I want to strangle someone, but I wouldn't change it for the world."

"You like it better than the narcotics unit?"

"Night and day difference. I'm not operating on a private vendetta here. Not that I regret my time with that unit."

Opening up to Jade felt natural. She made everything easy.

"The narcotics officer who discovered Sal's body delivered the news to my parents. That wasn't standard protocol. His name was Oliver Frank. Sal's death impacted him. He said he was tired of seeing kids dying before their twenty-first birthdays. He vowed to personally run down his murderer. To our grieving family, the fact that he cared about Sal meant a lot. He's the reason I decided to go into law enforcement."

"Did he find your brother's killer?"

His gut hardened. "He was gunned down in the line of duty before he could. I was in the patrol unit at the time. Once again, Frank impacted my career. I worked my way into narcotics and eventually started undercover gigs. I became obsessed with finding the men who'd taken both Sal's and Frank's lives and making them pay. After Denise and I were married, I was home maybe two months. She got fed up and left the week before our anniversary."

Jade's expression was difficult to read. "You never considered trying to win her back?"

"She remarried and has a kid."

"And what about you? Is your heart broken beyond repair?"

"Don't get me wrong. Her decision to quit, to walk out, tore me apart. Instead of fighting for our marriage, I went harder after revenge. I lost myself in that world. One night, I almost killed a man. Woke me up in a hurry. I felt like God was telling me that if I didn't give up this vendetta, it would destroy me. So, I walked away. Turned in my badge and service weapon and returned to the ranch. I worked from dawn until dusk for weeks on end, trying to stay busy so I didn't have to think about my failures."

Reliving the memories brought the disappointment and regret to the surface, and he had a scary thought.

He'd failed to get justice for Sal and for his own family. He'd failed to do the right thing for Denise. What if, after being so careful not to put himself into this sort of situation, he failed Jade and Henry, too?

After Jade had entered WITSEC, her handler had set her up with counseling sessions. The first thing her counselor had taught her was to take ownership of her mistakes. Cruz had been up front about the ones that had cost him his marriage and almost cost him his career. It was difficult to envision him living in the same world she'd inhabited, pretending to be ruthless and making terrible decisions in order to blend in. She understood how it must've torn him apart…craving justice for his brother but hating every minute of his false existence. And in the middle of that, his wife had walked out.

Jade was relieved he wasn't pining after Denise. The inconvenient truth? She wanted him for herself.

She returned Pumpkin to his cage. "How long did it take you?"

He cocked his head to one side. "For what?"

"To stop blaming yourself."

The skin around his eyes bunched, and he lowered his gaze. That was answer enough.

"You weren't there when your brother and that officer were killed. You didn't pack your wife's bags and ask for the house keys."

He caught his breath. "That's what my mom said. She gave me space initially, but that didn't last long. The woman has practically made lecturing into an art form."

Jade would like to meet the woman who'd raised this courageous, passionate, bighearted man.

"How long before you came to Tennessee?"

"I continued my undercover work for close to nine months after Denise left before resigning that first time. The department wanted me back, and I agreed, as long as no undercover was involved. But truly, my heart wasn't in it. I couldn't shake the disappointment. After another eighteen months, I saw the job opening for Serenity's mounted patrol officer, did some research into the position and the area, and cast my name in the pool."

"Your mom doesn't ask you to come back?"

"She's accepted that I'm content here. She says this is where God wants me."

His phone beeped with a text alert, and after reading it, he told Jade, "Officer Weiland just patrolled this area, and everything is quiet. He'll come this way again in another hour. Meanwhile, I'm hungry. What about you?"

"I could go for a salad."

"You don't want to take a walk on the wild side and have a burger?"

She tucked stray ends into the messy knot at the back of her head. "I will have some vegetable soup along with the salad."

"Can I talk you into chocolate mousse cake? We could share."

The image of them sharing a slice with one fork made her skin tingle. "I brought dessert."

He looked dubious. "Those things you made last night in the food processor?"

"Date balls."

"You put chia seeds in there. Along with other things I've never heard of. That's not dessert. What are cocoa nibs, anyway?"

Laughter bubbled up and spilled out.

"What's worse is you have poor Henry eating that stuff."

She laughed harder. Eventually his mock scowl gave way to amusement, and it reached his eyes. Oh, those eyes. They could turn her bones to jelly.

While he ordered their food on the Black Bear's website, she consulted the patient charts. The first round of meds was due to be administered soon.

As she read Pumpkin's dosage, the room was thrust into darkness.

"Cruz?"

He activated his phone light and no doubt saw the fear that had suddenly taken hold of her features. "Does the clinic have a generator?"

"No."

She tried to remain calm, but this had Axel's name written all over it.

"I want you to lock yourself in the bathroom." His hand closed over hers.

She resisted. "I can't leave the animals."

"This is just a precaution. Someone probably plowed into an electric pole."

"And if that isn't the case?"

"Axel doesn't care about the animals." His tone was grim.

She heard what he didn't say—Axel only wanted her.

He led her into the hallway, his phone light bouncing along the walls. They were almost to the bathroom when something was launched through the front door. Glass shattered, followed by a thud.

Cruz let go of her hand and unsheathed his weapon. "Change of plans."

They retraced their steps, turning right at the end of the hall and heading for the outdoor kennel. Already, some of the dogs were whining. Poor things. She couldn't act on her urge to comfort them.

He paused at the door. "Stay close to me."

Turning the lock, he pushed the door open.

"Evenin', Officer."

Axel greeted them with a rifle and a nauseating smile.

FIFTEEN

Axel's weapon dwarfed his own, but Cruz wasn't going to lower his. That would leave him and Jade at this man's mercy.

He shifted sideways to block her. "Appears we have a problem."

"I don't have a problem. You do."

The hair on Cruz's arms stood to attention. He reached behind him to pull Jade closer, but his fingers met empty space. Her gasp was accompanied by a fourth person's grunt.

"Go ahead," Axel taunted. "Have a look."

Sweat beaded on his forehead. Taking his eye off a loaded weapon pointed right at him went against common sense. Keeping his weapon trained on Axel, he peered over his shoulder.

A second man whose features were distorted by hosiery held a gun on Jade. Her eyes pleaded with Cruz to do something. He ran through various scenarios. Each and every one had a likely outcome—a bullet in Jade or himself, or both.

Fury bubbled like volcanic lava in his gut. He couldn't let Axel win. *Think, Cruz*.

"Where are the drugs you promised me?" the man holding a gun on Jade asked Axel. He sounded young and uncertain. Definitely inexperienced at the crime game. Cruz could use that to his advantage.

"When I'm done with you," Axel snapped. "Officer Castillo, toss your weapon in the grass."

Cruz didn't have a choice. As soon as he'd done so, Axel dug the rifle barrel into his chest and shoved him back a step. "Inside."

The turning of the lock felt like a death sentence. Axel had the upper hand. Weiland wouldn't be patrolling this way for another half hour, at least.

"Move."

Axel marched everyone into the surgical room, and Hose Man set a flashlight upright on the cabinets, illuminating the center of the room. The animals moved restlessly in their cages, and Pumpkin started mewling again.

Cruz and Jade stood side by side between Belinda's office and the hallway door.

"Get their phones."

Hose Man tucked his gun in his waistband and took Cruz's phone. Jade's was on the desk. He started to pocket them, but Axel snorted.

"Do you *want* the police to track you?"

He put the phones in the desk drawer. "Now what?"

"You brought the tape."

"Oh, yeah." The younger man reached into his pocket and produced a roll of silver duct tape. "You want me to tape their hands?"

"No, I want you to make a tape sculpture," Axel retorted, his hold on the rifle steady and assured. When Hose Man hesitated, Axel growled, "Tape their wrists as tight as possible."

Cruz observed him as he taped Jade's wrists together.

He was short and thin, an amateur. This was probably his first rodeo. He'd be easily bested.

Axel was another story. He'd had little else to do in prison other than pumping iron and learning to fight dirty. His distaste for law enforcement was exceeded only by his hatred for Jade.

Hose Man finished with Jade and turned to him.

"You sure you know what you're doing, kid?" Cruz murmured. "Helping an escaped felon?"

He hesitated. Cruz's muscles trembled with the need for action. He heeded that need, lodging his elbow in the man's Adam's apple and kicking his kneecap in one quick move. The man's howls bounced off the walls as he doubled over.

Cruz rushed Axel. He grabbed the rifle with both hands and pointed it to the ceiling. Axel refused to let go, and they wrestled over the weapon. Their momentum carried them into the cabinets, cracking the glass fronts and rattling the contents. Axel chopped the side of Cruz's neck with his flattened hand. He choked, and his eyes watered. A second blow in the same spot was enough to dislodge him.

In a blink, Axel brought the barrel sideways. When it connected with Cruz's skull, he saw stars bursting in the darkness and hit the floor on all fours. He almost vomited. Blackness swirled around him.

Lord, please don't let me lose consciousness.

Jade cried out for him, but Hose Man had recovered and held her back.

"Get up." Axel landed a swift kick to Cruz's ribs. He was pretty sure he felt one crack.

He sucked in short bursts of air, trying to rise above the pain and regroup. He couldn't give up.

He grasped the surgical table and climbed to his feet, leaning against it when his knees threatened to buckle.

"Stop! Just stop!" Jade pleaded, tugging against Hose Man's hold. "Do the right thing for once in your life, Axel. Forget this vendetta. Go live your life. Leave us alone."

"Forget?" he retorted. "Forget that my main girl played me for a fool? You know me, babe. No mercy, remember? I can't go back to my crew and tell them I let you off the hook."

"You could always lie," she challenged dryly.

"And miss out on the fun? I don't think so." He turned to his crony. "Take care of him."

Although clearly not the brightest bulb in the box, Hose Man bound Cruz's wrists tightly enough to cut off the blood supply to his hands. Having his hands fixed behind his back ramped up the pain in his side. Good. He needed the pain to keep him awake and alert. On the lookout for any opportunity to get Jade to safety.

Hose Man turned to Jade, who was leaning against the office door. "Where's the ketamine?"

"Cabinet closest to the desk."

He bounded over, busted out the glass with the butt of his gun and began stuffing the bottles into his pockets. Cruz shouldn't be surprised that the man had handed over human lives for a quick fix. Ketamine was popular in the drug scene. Since it couldn't easily be manufactured, users stole from vet clinics. Disgust coated his mouth.

"Leave one for me," Axel ordered, placing his rifle on the desk.

The implications of that command sent a shock wave through Cruz. His head whipped to Jade, whose features were horror-stricken.

"No, Axel." Jade edged toward the hallway.

He ignored her. Joining Hose Man, he told him to load a syringe for him.

Cruz started moving, too. If they could somehow get outside and flag a passerby, they might have a chance.

Axel happened to glance their way, and he muttered a string of expletives. Barreling across the room, he seized her arm and dragged her over to Hose Man. Cruz's blood boiled. He charged after them without a plan.

Axel snagged his cohort's gun and leveled it at Cruz. When Cruz halted, he went to the desk, hooked his foot around the chair leg and dragged it over.

"Sit."

Although every cell in his body rebelled, he did as ordered. If he got himself killed, he couldn't be of use to Jade. Axel kept the gun trained on him while Hose Man taped his ankles to the chair legs.

"Now can I go?" he whined.

With one clipped nod from Axel, the other man dashed out of the room, apparently uncaring that he'd left his weapon behind. The back door slammed shut. While Cruz liked that one foe had been removed from the equation, the situation was grim.

Axel shoved Jade to a seated position on the floor opposite Cruz and, stuffing the handgun in his waistband, crouched beside her. He wielded the syringe.

"Don't." Cruz's upper body strained forward, and the chair tipped over. He landed on his side, his cheek and temple glancing off the tile. The pain coursing through his body was nothing compared to what was unfolding before his eyes.

The brute trailed his fingers down her face. She cringed away from him, and he seized her chin, forcing eye contact. "Beautiful, feisty Jenny. You and I could've built an empire together. We could've been the king and queen of Gainesville. If only you hadn't ruined everything." His voice sharpened. "I wish I could stay and watch the show. The good officer here will be your only spectator."

She shook her head, her features a mask of terror. "Don't do this."

He shushed her and, maneuvering her head to one side, slid the needle in her neck and injected the liquid.

Cruz knew what God said about hating your enemies, but that was the only emotion he could manage at the moment. Hate and helplessness. He had never felt so helpless in all his life, not even when his parents had told him about Sal's death. What could he have done to change the outcome? Sal's cold, lifeless body had already been in the morgue.

Jade was still alive.

But for how long? an insidious voice prodded.

Axel pivoted and sneered at Cruz, his eyes tombs of evil. "You were a fool to think you'd beat me. Everyone who stands in my way will pay the price, one way or another."

He snatched his rifle from the table and used the same exit his partner had moments ago.

"Talk to me, Jade." He squirmed and shifted in an effort to reach her. "What can I do?"

Tears streamed down her face, and her eyes were closed. "Watch over my son," she whispered, each word punctuated with agony. "Tell him…" Her breathing was becoming labored. "Tell him I loved him."

"Look at me." He continued to try to get to her. The wooden chair was cumbersome and heavy.

She shook her head. "I can't." A sob quaked her shoulders, and her chin touched her chest, her hair streaming forward. "I can't bear it."

His chest squeezed, and his heart nearly ripped in two.

She thought he would judge her? Condemn her for something out of her control?

"I want to help you. Is there anything I can give you? Some medicine to counteract the ketamine?"

She didn't answer him. Instead, she slid slowly onto her side and pulled her knees up. "I can't think right now, Cruz. I'm going to sleep for a while."

Her voice had taken on a dreamy note, and he ground his teeth together. Even if there were something in this clinic that could help her, how would he reach it?

He kept going, desperate to get to her. It seemed to take ages, but he finally got within inches of her. Their heads were close together. He couldn't see her face, though, because of her hair.

"Hold on, Jade. Weiland will be here soon. Hold on for Henry's sake. For me, too."

It killed him to be this close to her and unable to touch her, rock her in his arms and promise her everything was going to be okay.

A soft sigh left her lips. "You're cute, you know that? My fiery Texan."

Cruz squeezed his eyes shut. He didn't want to hear that from her unless she was in her right mind.

"I'm going to try and reach the phones."

"Don't leave me," she murmured, unmoving.

"I wouldn't dream of it, darlin'."

He started praying for stamina and guidance. This was going to be nigh on impossible. Before he'd made the first move, he heard the crunch of glass.

"Cruz? You in there?"

He recognized the Black Bear waitress's voice. "Paige!" he called out. "Call an ambulance!"

Thank You, Lord. He'd ordered the food right before Axel got there. *Thank You for sending help.*

Paige entered the room and promptly dropped the paper sacks.

"Call 911," he repeated. "Then look in that desk for scissors or a knife you can use to free us."

Her mouth opened and closed. She fumbled for her cell phone and contacted dispatch. He told her what to tell them. Without ending the connection, she placed the phone on the floor and riffled through the drawers.

"Found it." The college student dashed over, her eyes as huge as the plates they used to serve their onion blossom appetizer. "What now?"

Cruz relayed his wishes, urging her to act quickly. "I don't care if you nick me. Time is not on our side."

Paige managed to slice through the tape with only a few minor cuts to his wrists. As soon as he was free, he flexed his fingers to get the blood pumping. He dispensed with the tape around his ankles and, kicking the chair away, went to work on Jade's restraints.

When her arms were free, he tucked her hair behind her ear and cupped her face.

"Help is on the way, darlin'."

Her mouth curved in an exaggerated smile. She tried to lift her finger to his nose but couldn't. Her eyes were glazed, her pupils dilated.

Her unfocused gaze bounced around the room. Did she recognize him or her surroundings? Or had her mind succumbed to the substance coursing through her veins?

He'd heard of people dying from a ketamine overdose on rare occasions. Had Axel given her a lethal amount? His heart quaked with denial.

Jade couldn't die. She couldn't. Henry needed her.

He told Paige to stay with her. Grabbing both their phones from the desk, he retrieved his gun from the outdoor kennel and returned to Jade's side. He sat on the floor and held her hand, wishing he could pour his strength into her.

"Is she going to be okay?" Paige asked, hovering nearby.

"The effects aren't long-lasting. Maybe an hour or two, depending on a variety of factors." Depending on how much was in her system.

The helpless feeling returned. He wanted nothing more than to rewind time and handle things differently. He'd failed her, just like he'd failed Sal and Denise.

The ambulance's siren was the sweetest sound he'd heard in hours.

"You came at the right time, Paige. You're an answer to prayer."

Jade didn't flinch as the sirens permeated the building, stirring the animals into a frenzy. She was unresponsive as the paramedics strapped her to the gurney. Cruz was literally shaking by the time they got her loaded into the vehicle. They rejected his request to ride with her. He could've pressed the issue, but she wouldn't know he was there anyway. He needed the solitary ride to the hospital to calm down.

Powerful, soul-shaking emotions bombarded him. He fought to regain control. He didn't want to care this deeply. Wasn't ready to risk his heart again. Not for anyone, not even Jade.

She was being pulled deep under the waves, a manacle around her wrist holding her fast. Her lungs begged for relief. Startled awake, she found herself in a dim, sterile room. The whoosh and whisper of the ocean rolled from a speaker. Out of place here, yet it explained her dream. Her skin was tight and itchy, and her head throbbed. When she tried to lift her hand, she met resistance.

The manacle. Was she handcuffed to the bed?

Her heart fluttering in panic, she tugged harder. Something—no, someone—shifted in the chair. The fingers around her wrist began to stroke her sensitive skin. She got a whiff of Cruz's distinct scent and turned her head on the thin pillow.

The expression on his bruised face was hard to decipher. The memories of what happened at the clinic slammed into her, making her gasp. She bolted upright. Her stomach swooshed sideways.

"Are you in pain?" He stood, one hand cradling his ribs.

"I'm not taking any more drugs, legal or not," she said hotly.

Humiliation and denial crawled over her skin like tiny spiders. She'd vowed to herself that she wouldn't ever lose herself like that again. Lose time. Lose control.

For this to happen at all was her worst nightmare. For Cruz to witness it? Beyond words.

She buried her face in her hands.

The tears didn't come. She felt hollow. Her hope? Gone.

Why did this happen, God? You know my struggles, how difficult it was to rise out of the ashes. You remember my commitment to a clean, upright life. All I wanted was to raise my son in this peaceful mountain town and leave Axel and my bad choices behind.

He cleared his throat. "The doctor said it's unlikely you'll experience cravings. Ketamine isn't as addictive as other substances."

She lifted her head. He'd backed away, almost to the door, and he stood with his hands at his sides. He looked miserable. Or was he uncomfortable being around her?

Her heart thrummed with indignation. "The day I had my first ultrasound and saw my baby, I vowed I wouldn't put anything in my body that would harm him. I checked out library books and read blogs about nutrition. I traded coffee for smoothies, sugary cereals for oatmeal, candy bars for date balls. After he was born, my convictions strengthened. He was entirely dependent on me, and I wouldn't have jeopardized his well-being for anything. I've stuck to that vow." Her hands twisted the crisp, abrasive sheets. "I refuse to let Axel or anyone else derail me."

His expression shuttered even more, and his gaze slid to his boots. She suddenly wished him gone. In the clinic, he'd risked his life to try and save her. He'd obviously had time to mull over what happened. He was acting as if she was the girl she used to be...

She squeezed her eyes shut, gripped with embarrassment. While under the influence, how had she acted? Looked? Talked? All she knew was that, more than anything, she'd craved this man's approval.

Be real. You wanted far more than that.

Clearly, from his body language, she would be getting neither.

"Why are you still here, Cruz?"

His forehead furrowed, and something sparked in his eyes. "Where else would I be?"

"You obviously want to be anywhere else but here."

"That's not true—"

A knock announced a nurse's arrival, and he clamped his mouth shut. The pretty young brunette checked her vitals and announced she was free to leave.

Jade was tempted to call Tessa and ask her to pick her up. Tessa would be happy to take her and Henry in, as would Lindsey and Raven. But that would invite questions and potentially put Cruz in a tough spot with his sergeant and fellow officers, not to mention confuse and upset Henry even further.

She was resilient. She could handle his silent condemnation.

This was a timely reminder that caring for the Texan wasn't wise. He would never reciprocate her feelings. Besides, she didn't need a man who lost faith in her so easily.

She swung her feet around to the floor, and the room tilted. He moved to assist her, but she held him off. The sensation gradually faded.

"Who's caring for the animals? They need meds and fluids, not to mention lots of reassurance. They can't be left alone. Did you get my phone? I have to contact Belinda."

"Already taken care of. I called her on the way here and explained everything. She was heading straight over to the clinic."

Jade kneaded her forehead. "Those poor animals..."

"The important thing is none of them were hurt."

He was right. "Can you wait out in the hall?"

Surprise flickered across his face. "You might not be steady on your feet after..."

His words trailed off, riling her.

"After I was pumped full of ketamine?"

He grimaced and looked away.

"Just go."

He turned on his booted heel and closed the door softly behind him. It was wrong that she felt disappointed, that she had wanted him to ignore her words, take her into his arms and hold her. When she glimpsed her reflection in the bathroom's unforgiving lights, she almost broke down. She'd looked the same after a night of partying.

Messy hair. Bloodshot eyes. Smeared mascara. Dry, cracked lips.

She gripped the porcelain sink and willed the tears away.

"I didn't choose this," she said aloud.

She couldn't let the creeping shame take root. Couldn't let Axel destroy her.

Refocused, she donned her dirty scrubs because they were all she had and stepped out into the hall.

Cruz was silent during the long walk through the hospital. Once inside his truck, he blasted the heater and turned on the radio but still did not speak. The tension inside the cab was almost unbearable. She wanted to rail at him. How dare he condemn her?

The fact he'd opened his home to her and Henry without complaint and had risked his life for hers kept her silent.

Her relief was significant when his house came into view. Outside fixtures lit up the yard, and the living room windows gleamed a soft yellow. He ushered her in—close but not touching, fortunately—deactivated the alarm, and offered her drinks and food. She declined and ducked into the bathroom, desperate to wash away the grime. If only she could wash away tonight's events with soap and water.

When she emerged, he was waiting in the hallway with an oversize mug of hot herbal tea.

"Better?"

She wrapped both hands around the mug and inhaled the scents of honey, lemon and ginger. He watched her sip the tea, his unwavering focus doing strange things to her equilibrium.

"Much better." She held the mug close to her chest and ordered her body to behave. "Did a doctor check your injuries?"

"Nothing major. Bruised ribs."

Lights flashed through the living room windows, followed by a car door slamming.

Uneasiness swirled through her. "Who's that?"

"I hope you don't mind," he said, hesitating. "I asked her to come."

She trailed him into the living room, curiosity warring with dread. She wasn't up for company.

He opened the door and moved aside. Her best friend stood on the porch.

"Leslie!"

Leslie enveloped her in a hug, and the dam holding back Jade's emotions crumbled into bits. Tears flooded her cheeks, and sobs shook her body. When Leslie led her to the couch and offered her a package of tissues from her purse, Jade noticed Cruz had disappeared.

"What did Cruz tell you?"

"Only that you needed me." Leslie's eyes brimmed with concern and questions.

"He's right. I do." She blew her nose and swiped at her cheeks.

She couldn't believe he'd done this for her. It didn't change anything between them, however. He wasn't the man God had in mind for her, and she certainly wasn't his new lease on life.

SIXTEEN

"You've made my taste buds dance in anticipation," Leslie said as Cruz slid a plate in front of her Saturday morning. She took a big whiff. "What's this called again?"

"*Machacado*. Shredded dried beef, scrambled eggs and *pico de gallo*. I added shredded cheese. It's the only breakfast my mom taught me to make. She had to twist my arm to get me in the kitchen. Now that I don't have frequent access to her cooking, I regret my laziness."

His smile was strictly for Leslie's benefit. Jade's friend was astute. Did she sense the undercurrent of tension passing between them?

"Yogurt and granola for you, as requested." He set a bowl before her.

"I would like to try your dish," she said, determined to be pleasant. She was a guest in his home, after all. An unwanted guest. "But I'm not sure what my stomach can handle this morning."

She'd wakened with a slight headache and a general feeling of unwellness. That could be due to the ketamine's lingering effects or lack of sleep. She and Leslie had talked for hours last night, crying, hugging and praying.

His gaze lingered on her. "I'll fix it again another day."

Leslie took a bite and hummed loudly. "Okay, now my

taste buds are doing the salsa. You could charge for this, you know."

Over at the stove, Cruz scooped a hefty portion for himself. "I'm glad you like it."

He returned to the table, wincing as he sat in the chair across from them, and picked up his fork. Mottled bruising covered his cheek. Jade had a flashback of him bound to the chair, of it crashing to the floor, of Axel's boot aiming for his ribs.

A lump formed in her throat.

"You should be resting today," she blurted. "Not waiting on us."

Cruz didn't look up from his plate. "I'm not letting you loose in my kitchen," he quipped. "You're likely to sneak dates in my food."

Laughter shook Leslie's shoulders. "Smart man. If you're not careful, she'll have you eating hockey pucks for breakfast."

Jade elbowed her. "You're being melodramatic. My pumpkin-oat muffins are tasty and good for you."

Leslie pointed her fork at Cruz. "Hockey pucks."

He changed the subject by inviting Leslie to talk about her family. He exuded an interested air, but his gaze repeatedly returned to his phone and occasionally to the windows. Clearly, he hadn't forgotten the reason he had guests to feed.

Jade's stomach tightened. She swirled the granola through the yogurt, her appetite nonexistent. Where was Axel? It was too much to hope he'd left town, satisfied with his victory. Knowing him, he'd stuck around to make sure he'd finished the job. Or maybe this was his way of toying with her.

"I had plans to visit Texas between Christmas and the

new year," Cruz was saying, "but I'm not sure if I will go or not."

Jade looked at him, and he covered the moment with a long sip of coffee.

"If you go," Leslie told him, "I'll pay you to bring back some of your mama's cooking. Or even better, her recipes."

Leslie launched into a conversation about her own family's favorite foods, all of which Jade had sampled at one time or another. When they'd finished eating, Leslie received a call from her son and excused herself. Jade carried the dishes to the sink. Before Cruz could start rinsing them, she put her hand on his arm.

His dark eyes all but consumed her, causing her heart to trip over itself.

She withdrew her fingers as if his skin was a hot griddle. "You knew exactly what I needed. I can't thank you enough."

"She's important to you."

"Leslie is a special woman, and I'm grateful God brought her into my life."

She was grateful for Cruz, too, despite how things stood between them.

The doorbell rang. "That will be Mason and Tessa," he said, drying off his hands and letting them in.

Henry raced straight for Jade, his face beaming. "Mommy, guess what? We had blueberry pancakes for breakfast!"

She knelt and enveloped him in a hug, overwhelmed with gratitude. Henry could have been without a mother this morning, had God not kept His hand of protection on her.

He wouldn't have been alone, however. Every single person in this house would have made sure he was loved and cared for.

Unaware of her deep thoughts, Henry wiggled out of her arms. "Lily's going to get a hamster for Christmas," he claimed. "And I got to sleep in her tepee."

"Is that right?"

Mason and Tessa were in conversation with Cruz. Lily was tucked in her daddy's arms, her head on his shoulder and big eyes surveying the room.

Leslie emerged from the bedroom and greeted Henry with a giant smile. He ran into her open arms, and she dispensed with an exaggerated bear hug.

Mason and Tessa had met Leslie before, and they came over to greet her.

Henry tugged on her blouse sleeve. "Are you going to be at my birthday party?"

Her dark eyes met Jade's in question. "I haven't missed one yet, young man."

Jade sighed. She would have to speak to Henry today and explain that the arcade party he'd begged for wasn't going to happen, after all.

Cruz stepped close beside her, his fingers skimming her back. She shivered, his touch shimmering up and down her spine. It wasn't enough. It was never enough.

"Can I talk to you for a moment?"

"Uh, sure."

They moved into the hallway near his bedroom. "I have an idea for an alternative birthday celebration and thought I'd run it by you before I take it to Mason."

Surprised, she gestured for him to go on.

"Henry loves horses. What if we decorated the stables and set up cake and presents in the break room? Ten kids and their families would be too many, but I thought Lily and Kai could be there. Security wouldn't be an issue. The horses don't mind noise or balloons, of course." He shifted his stance, his expression somber. "What do you think? Not as exciting as an arcade, but it could work."

"He does love horses."

"He'd be the first kid ever to have his birthday party at the mounted police stables."

She shouldn't be surprised that he'd given thought to her son's happiness. Throughout this whole ordeal, Cruz had been wonderful with Henry. Of course, Henry wasn't the one he had a problem with.

"It's perfect. Thank you, Cruz."

For a brief instant, sadness shone in his eyes. He recovered quickly, though, inclining his head and returning to the group.

What did he have to be sad about?

Cruz felt like he'd been stomped on by an angry bull. He walked stiffly between the trees behind the vet clinic, his gaze scanning the carpet of dead leaves and pine needles, hoping to find something linked to Axel's accomplice. Hose Man was probably a local. Running him down just might lead them to their man.

He turned to glance back at the clinic, his ribs angry at the inconsiderate movement. Raven stopped her search lower down the hill and raised her brows. "You should be at home with Jade."

That was the last place he should be. After the others had left, she and Henry had settled on the couch, cozied beneath a blanket, and turned on a Christmas movie. Henry had asked him to join them. Jade's eyes had been telling. She didn't want him to stay.

He knew exactly what she thought of him. And even though it was eating him up inside, he wasn't going to correct her assumptions. This distance between them was necessary. He couldn't let his feelings for her grow any more than they already had.

Desperate for a reprieve from the cozy living room scene, he'd called Bell and asked him to guard the house so he could help SPD with the search. Mason had decided to postpone the drone training scheduled for today.

Raven bent to examine a broken branch, her thick braid swinging forward over her shoulder. "Jade seems to be doing okay."

Leslie hadn't been gone ten minutes before the rest of his unit and their significant others had descended on his house. Jade had gotten teary-eyed amid all the hugs and encouragement. His friends had rallied around her, and he appreciated that more than he could say. It was as if, by supporting her, they were supporting him, as well. But he and Jade weren't a team or a couple. Never would be.

"She's a fighter."

Raven straightened. "I'm glad you took lead on her case."

"Why?"

"You need her."

Hands hanging at his sides, he stared at her. "Why?"

"If you have to ask, you've been alone too long, my friend."

"Here's the problem. The three of you are thick in the middle of marital bliss, and you want me to drink the same punch. I'm not getting married again. Period." He didn't care how beautiful, sweet and loving Jade was or what kind of reaction she caused inside him each time she came near.

"Who said anything about marriage?" Her eyes sparkled.

He rolled his eyes and started walking again. His head throbbed with each step.

Raven wasn't done, though. "Your personalities complement each other beautifully. She's grounded, calm and smooths your rough edges."

He grunted. Calmness wasn't the reaction she aroused in him.

"Young Henry has taken a shine to you. You'd make a wonderful dad to him and any other kiddos that came along."

"How about you focus on your own relationship?" he snapped, irritated that her rambling created images of dark-haired, green-eyed babies. He was *not* going to daydream about having children with Jade. "When are you and Aiden going to start a family?"

Her cheeks pinked. "I'd like to have him all to myself for a while before we start our family."

Cruz's ire cooled. He supposed he could understand why his friends wanted him to find love. If he had what they had, he'd want the people he cared about to experience similar happiness.

"Castillo! We got something!"

He and the others converged on the far corner of the fence line. Weiland held an evidence bag aloft. Inside was the hosiery Axel's accomplice had been wearing.

Raven touched his elbow. "Think he was smart enough to wash it first?" she asked sarcastically.

"If only we could get the DNA results in hours rather than days." Or even weeks.

"We're not gonna sit on our hands while we wait," she reminded him. "Between SPD, the sheriff's department, and our FBI and marshal friends, we'll identify this guy, and he'll lead us to Axel."

"I wish I had your confidence."

"I know God's on our side. Remember my favorite verse."

"'But without faith it is impossible to please Him, for

he that cometh to God must believe that He is, and that He is a rewarder of them that diligently seek Him.'"

She had it plastered on her locker and framed on her office desk.

Cruz found himself praying for faith. The faith to trust in God's plan. He prayed for strength and wisdom to protect Jade. And to guard his heart until this case was over.

SEVENTEEN

Monday morning, at last. Five days until Christmas. Jade stared out the window at the passing houses adorned with cheerful ribbons, wreaths and snowmen, her fingers combing through her scarf fringes. Normally she'd be making the trek to town alone on a weekday. After dropping Henry at a sitter's or school, she'd head straight to the clinic. But the clinic was closed today for cleaning and repair work, and, she reminded herself, she had been put on leave. Belinda and David had brought flowers to her at Cruz's on Saturday evening and apologized profusely for not having an alarm at the clinic. They were understandably shocked that the robbers had injected her with ketamine. Of course, they didn't know about her past or her connection to Axel. And she'd kept it that way.

Cruz had excused himself during that portion of the conversation. Her heart squeezed painfully.

Turning her head, she observed his profile. If he sensed her gaze, he didn't show it. He kept his attention on the road ahead, gloved hands propped on his thighs and fingers on the wheel. His black jacket collar was turned up, skimming the underside of his chin.

He'd avoided her most of yesterday. After watching online church services with her and Henry—because attend-

ing in person carried too much risk—he'd shared a hastily
assembled lunch and then descended into his downstairs
retreat. Henry had gotten curious and ventured down there.
She'd heard conversation and, later, a television program.
She hadn't gone to investigate.

The chasm between them shouldn't hurt this much. She
regretted giving him the power to hurt her. Her fault, of
course. Cruz hadn't let on that he had feelings for her. He'd
been the consummate professional.

Though she suspected he'd rather be far from her, he
kept her at his side today as they rode toward town.

Up ahead, right before a mom-and-pop gas station, a
cruiser with flashing lights waited on the road's shoulder.
A beat-up hatchback sat at an angle, partly on the asphalt
and partly in the yellowed grass. Cruz slowed the truck
and parked behind it. She could see a man's silhouette in
the back.

Officer Bell had called and informed Cruz that he'd discovered a bottle of ketamine during a routine traffic stop.
Since they'd already dropped Henry at Elaine's, they'd
driven straight over.

Tucking her scarf deeper into her coat, she exited the
truck. The morning air was brisk and scented with pine.
The thick cloud cover hung close above their heads, blocking the sun.

Officer Bell met her and Cruz in the space between
their vehicles.

"I pulled him over for a broken taillight. He was agitated, and his car reeks of weed. I conducted a search and
found this."

Bell held a bottle in his gloved hand. "The prescription
label has been scratched off. I tested the contents. Positive for ketamine."

Cruz looked at Jade. "Is this from the clinic?"

"It looks like ours."

Bell's gaze tracked a passing garbage truck. "I already checked with vets in surrounding towns, and none of them have had recent thefts."

Cruz gestured to the cruiser. "He tell you where he scored this?"

"He hasn't said much."

"Because he's under the influence?" Cruz said sharply.

Bell shook his head. "Seems relatively sober to me. It's more of not wanting to snitch."

"Has he been in trouble before?" Jade asked, shivering when the wind gusted and whipped at her hair.

"This is his first offense." Bell set the ketamine on the trunk beside a test kit. "His name is Kent Myers. I'm sure you know his mom, Cruz. She's a waitress at the Black Bear. Been there for years."

"Vickie?" Cruz squinted at the rear window.

"That's the one."

He groaned. "Vickie's a sweetheart. She brags on her son every chance she gets. She's gonna be devastated. Why do these kids continue to make dumb decisions?"

"For a lot of reasons," Jade shot back. "Or none at all."

Bell's gaze bounced between them before he opened the rear door and assisted the young man outside. His clothes were disheveled, and his honey-blond hair hung in his eyes.

Jade bit down hard on her lip. He couldn't have been more than twenty. If not for the dark circles under his eyes and belligerent glare, he would've been handsome.

"I'm not a squealer," he snarled.

His gaze snagged on her, and his brow furrowed, no doubt confused by her presence. She offered a tremulous smile. His eyes widened before sliding to his feet.

"You scratch our back, we'll scratch yours," Cruz said. There was no response.

"We need a name. Who sold you the K?"

Kent scuffed his untied shoe against the pavement.

Cruz folded his arms over his chest. "What are you? A senior in high school?"

"Yeah. So?"

"Your record is clean. Adding a drug charge is going to make it harder to get into college or the military."

"Who cares?"

His tough attitude was belied by the hint of worry in his voice.

"You think Patrick in the gas station here will be eager to hire you? How could he trust you to run the cash register? You'd be fortunate if he trusts you to clean his bathrooms."

When he didn't respond, Cruz shrugged. "Have it your way. We'll take you in and call Vickie. Or should you be the one to tell her? You do get a phone call."

Kent's head whipped up. "You know my mom?"

"Sweet lady. I'm a regular at the café. She talks about you a lot. Of course, she probably won't want to share this with the customers."

The boy licked his lips, his expression panicked. "I scored it off a guy who comes around the high school. He used to go there."

Bell pulled out his notebook. "Name?"

"Scott Pelt."

"He's on our radar," Bell told Cruz.

"Thought it sounded familiar. Where does he live, Kent?"

"I don't know, I swear. He hangs out in the athletic park near the school. That's where students meet up with him."

Cruz's eyes were black with outrage. A rock thrown at his jaw would bounce off, it was so rigid.

Kent shivered beneath that glare. "You're not going to tell him who told you, are you?"

"No, but I will be having a talk with your mom."

"Hey—"

"And giving another speech at the high school. Looks like I'll have to up my game."

Bell unlocked Kent's handcuffs. "Don't let me catch you with drugs in your possession again. No more second chances, you hear?"

The boy nodded shakily and, with one last glance at Cruz, hurried to his car. The engine sputtered to life, and he drove away. Bell got into his cruiser to access his computer, leaving her and Cruz alone for a moment.

"I can talk to the students," Jade offered before fully thinking it through.

Cruz turned to stare, his lips parting.

The more she thought about it, the more she was convinced she could help. She should at least try. "What good is my past if I don't use it to point others in the right direction? If I can stop one kid from taking the same path, it would be worth it."

Why hadn't he thought of this before? Not Jade, specifically, but someone who could speak from personal experience. The students were much more likely to listen to a civilian who'd overcome poor lifestyle choices than they were a cop.

Before he could answer, Bell returned with Scott Pelt's address.

"How do you want to play it?"

"We'll need backup on the off chance Scott's not alone. I'll ask Mason to meet us there."

"I'll reach out to Weiland," Bell said. "What about our FBI and marshal friends?"

"We'll contact them if this pans out."

Distracted, he placed his hand against Jade's back as they returned to the truck. Her sharp inhale reminded him of his place.

I'm a cop. She's a citizen in trouble. A case number. Nothing more.

He climbed behind the wheel, careful not to tax his sore ribs, and texted Mason. Pulling onto the road behind Bell, he told Jade, "Mason's set to meet us at the Wingate apartment complex. You'll have to stay in the truck until we secure the suspect."

"All right."

Her voice was soft, almost sad. He glanced over. Her charcoal-gray peacoat and multicolored scarf enhanced her eyes. Sparkly silver clasps were tucked into her hair above her left ear, while the rest flowed unchecked down her back. Miniature silver tree earrings winked in her earlobes. Her fingernails shimmered a forest green.

He was used to seeing her in scrubs. While those weren't boring—some were neon hues and some had playful prints—this outfit was dressy. Festive, even.

Celebrating the holiday season was far from her mind, he was certain. Did she, like him, keep replaying Friday's chaotic scenes? Did she relive the helplessness and frustration? The not knowing if they would live to see another sunrise?

Gritting his teeth, he turned up the radio and studied the passing scenery. Weiland was already at the complex when they parked. Mason joined them ten minutes later.

Bell showed them a photograph of their guy. Cruz wasn't able to positively identify him, thanks to the hosiery disguise Axel's accomplice had worn, but Scott did fit the body weight and height categories.

Cruz scoped out the complex. Should he leave Jade in

the truck? She would be far from the action. Vulnerable, though. He was second-guessing his decisions, and that didn't bode well.

He opened her door. "Come with us. You can hang back, out of sight."

The group hemmed her in as they crossed the lot, bypassing the office and several buildings to reach the last one on this row. Each two-story section was comprised of eight apartments, with a central, outdoor staircase. Pulling their weapons, they climbed the metal stairs to the second story and approached the right rear unit.

Cruz motioned to Weiland to stay back and guard Jade. The officer nodded and maneuvered her close to the building.

Bell pounded on the door, referred to as a cop knock—one that could alert the neighbors.

They heard muttering and footsteps. The door cracked open to reveal a bleary-eyed, sandy-haired man. "What do you want?"

"Scott Pelt? My colleagues and I have some questions for you."

The authoritative tone, along with the uniforms and guns, jolted the man awake. He shoved on the door. Bell stopped it with his foot and advanced into the apartment. Cruz was right behind him, and Mason held up the rear.

Scott tripped over a garbage can and sprawled on the carpet. "You can't do this. I haven't done anything."

Bell held his weapon aloft while Cruz and Mason cleared the rooms. When they deemed it safe, Bell holstered his gun and hauled Scott to his feet. He pointed to the couch.

"Sit."

Mason began to look around the kitchen. "Bingo."

When he held up three bottles of ketamine, Scott paled.

Cruz's pulse thundered in his ears. Stepping between the coffee table and the couch, he loomed over Scott. "Where were you Friday night between the hours of 6:00 and 8:00 p.m.?"

Scott looked up, for the first time seeming to notice the mottled bruising on Cruz's cheek. His lips pulled back in fear, revealing uneven front teeth. He visibly swallowed.

Mason cleared his throat. "Holster your weapon, Cruz."

"I was here, man," Scott said. "Some friends came over to party."

"Don't lie to me." The clinic attack fresh in his mind, he started to lean in.

"Cruz," Mason barked. "Your gun."

Scott stared up at him with wide eyes. Cruz blew out a breath, counted to ten and obeyed his superior officer's command. Weapon secured, he leaned in.

"We found the hose disguise outside the clinic. It's only a matter of time before the DNA results are in. Let's try this again. Where were you Friday night?"

Beads of sweat popped out on his forehead.

"I was there, okay? I needed the score. But I didn't hurt you or your lady friend, remember? I didn't lay a hand on you."

"No, you helped the man who did hurt us." Fury built inside him. Jade could have died. "Between that and the ketamine, you're going away for a very long time."

Cruz kicked the coffee table leg. Bell and Mason stared at him, brows raised, silently asking if they needed to take over.

"I didn't know what he had planned, you know."

"You didn't care," Cruz growled, glaring down at him. "Where is Axel now?"

"I swear, I don't know."

"Where'd you meet him?"

"The Rusty Nail. He approached me. Asked if I wanted to make some money and score some K."

"When?"

"Thursday night. He told me to meet him Friday afternoon at the bar. When I got there, he gave me a handgun and explained what he wanted. I haven't seen him since that night."

Mason propped his boot on the couch cushion. "Did he say where he's staying?"

"No."

"Did you see what he was driving?"

"A black truck." He gave them the make and model. "The windshield was cracked."

Mason immediately got on the phone with dispatch.

Bell got the handcuffs ready. "Anything else you can think of that will help us locate him?"

"Can't we make a deal here or something?" Scott whined. "I told you what I know."

Cruz swallowed his retort and stalked outside.

"Nothing unusual out here," Weiland said before handing off Jade and heading inside.

Jade pushed off from the wall, her expression hopeful. Cruz wished he had more to offer, to keep her hope alive.

"We got a make and model, so we're putting out a BOLO for the vehicle Axel was using Friday," he told her.

Her expression fell. "He could've already ditched it."

"It's a possibility. But if he doesn't think we can track down his buddy Scott, he'll keep using it."

A breeze teased the ends of her platinum hair. She put her hands together and blew on them. He pulled his gloves off.

"Take mine."

She stared at the gloves, then lifted her gaze to his. "No, thanks."

He hadn't realized she had a stubborn streak. Or maybe she wasn't in the mood to accept any kind gestures from him. "Please?"

She took the gloves and put them on. They engulfed her small hands, of course, but they'd keep her fingers warm. "What happens now?"

"The feds and marshals are going to be all over this new info. They'll search for Axel."

"He's managed to evade authorities this long. What makes you think that will change now?"

"We have to stay positive, Jade. If not for ourselves, for Henry."

She bit down hard on her lip, shook her head and stared at nothing. He yearned to comfort her with more than words. Instead, he stuffed his hands in his pockets.

He was not what she needed or what she wanted, he reminded himself.

The rift he'd allowed to grow between them would have to remain intact.

EIGHTEEN

Her baby was six years old.

That evening, Jade placed the decorated cake on the table and watched Henry's smile stretch from ear to ear, his big green eyes reflecting the shimmering candles. As the birthday song swelled in the stables' break room, the deeper, smoother adult voices blending with the children's high-pitched ones, she was overwhelmed with God's goodness.

Although she didn't deserve the blessings He'd showered upon her, she was deeply grateful. *Thank You, Jesus.*

Jade carved the cake into slices and placed them on colorful paper plates. Elaine doled them out to the kids first and then the officers and other adults. When everyone had cake, Jade retreated to the drinks station at the back wall and poured herself a glass of lemon water. The break room was outfitted with a fridge, upper and lower cabinets, and a sink. A microwave and coffee maker sat on the counter.

"You forgot to serve yourself." Tessa joined her, holding out a plate of cake. "You have to try this."

Jade accepted the plate and dutifully took a bite, even though she had zero appetite. The chocolate cake with fudge glaze had the perfect amount of sweetness. When she'd called the bakery to order Henry's cake, she'd asked for something that wouldn't make their teeth ache. "This is good."

"It's delicious," Tessa agreed. "I might have to order this for Mason's birthday."

They could see the entire room from their vantage point. The adults had to wade through the bobbing balloons and repeatedly bat them away. Streamers dripped from the walls. Every color of the rainbow was represented in the tablecloths and coordinated plates, napkins, cups and forks.

"Sending Mason, Cruz and Silver to the party supply store might've been a mistake," Jade said, smiling wryly. "Do you think they left anything for the other customers?"

"According to Mason, this is all on Cruz. He had no self-control." Tessa laughed. "They all want Henry to have the best birthday ever."

Cruz was crouched beside Henry's chair and listening intently to whatever he was saying. How odd it was that, in such a short time, Cruz had become integral to her happiness. He'd come to matter to her and her son.

She allowed herself to appreciate how his navy-hued SMP shirt enhanced his golden skin and midnight hair and molded to his strong shoulders and muscular back. Then she cut the thoughts off and turned her focus to her son.

"I can't believe he's six. I still remember how he looked when he was first born. He was crying when the nurse placed him in my arms. I was terrified." She paused, remembering all the birthdays since then. Some had been easier than others. "The years seem to have gone by in a blink."

"I know how you feel."

Jade and Tessa had both had their babies without the support of family. Both had raised their children alone under stressful circumstances. Tessa's story had a happy ending—she'd reconciled with the father of her child, and they were raising Lily together. That wasn't possible for Jade.

"I have big hopes for my boy," she said, shoving the futile thoughts away. "I want him to follow his dreams. I want him to be happy and fulfilled. Most importantly, I want him to love Jesus and follow Him with all his heart."

Tessa squeezed her arm. "You're doing it right, Jade. He's precious. I confess, I sometimes like to think he and Lily might wind up together."

Jade grinned. "Then you and I would officially be family."

Tessa's brow creased. "You already are my family."

"Stop that. You're going to make me cry."

She'd spent so much time crying during this season that was supposed to be joyful. Tears of fear, frustration, anger and sadness. Today was a celebration.

Leslie separated from the group and ventured over. "I need your baker's name."

Jade finished off her last bite and told her about the bakery. "I'm glad I took Lindsey's advice and went there."

"Henry doesn't seem upset about the change in his birthday plans," Leslie said, watching him.

"The Serenity Mounted Police aim to serve and, in this case, save a little boy's birthday."

"Cruz instigated this whole thing," Tessa said, pouring herself a decaffeinated soda.

They watched as Cruz grinned at Henry and patted his arm.

Leslie let out a satisfied grunt. "He cares about Henry as if he's his own son."

Jade pressed her lips together. He was clearly fond of Henry. But he wasn't looking to be part of a family again, and definitely not with her.

"Can we open presents now, Mommy?" Henry called out to her.

Jade nodded. She pasted on a smile and chose the first paper-wrapped box from the gift table she passed.

"That one's from me," Cruz told Henry, his dark eyes fastened on Jade.

Did he realize how he looked at her sometimes? Like she was a source of fascination? Like he couldn't decide if he trusted her or not?

Henry ripped open the paper and cheered. Cruz had gotten him an art set with markers, crayons, colored pencils and stickers.

Henry peered up at him. "Can we draw more animals?"

"You can count on it, cowboy."

Kai and Lily pressed in on either side of Henry's chair, exclaiming over each gift he opened. When he'd revealed the final one, Cruz clapped his hands together.

"Who's ready to give the horses treats?"

The kids jumped up and down, each eagerly taking an apple and trailing Cruz out of the room. Jade got her phone ready to take pictures. In the stable area, everyone waited along one side while Cruz, Silver and Mason led the horses out of their stalls.

Jade's jaw dropped. Each horse looked like they were about to take part in a royal parade. Their manes and tails were woven with ribbons of all shades. Pinks, yellows, greens, blues. The kids gazed at them in awe.

Raven nudged her shoulder. "Stunning, isn't it?"

"Did you do this?"

Her black brows winged up. "Me? I don't have the patience. While you and Henry were hiding out in the meeting room earlier and Silver, Mason and I were decorating the break room, Cruz was out here prettying up the horses."

She blinked. Cruz grinned as he boosted Henry onto Renegade's back. She'd never seen him this relaxed before.

"Are you sure?"

"Why is it so difficult for you to believe? He adores your son. He's good with kids in general. I keep telling him to find a wife already and start a family. He's hard-headed, though."

There was something in her tone that brought Jade's gaze back to her. "What aren't you saying?"

She shrugged, her honey-colored eyes twinkling. "I don't know what you mean."

"You don't think that he and I…"

"Why not? It's obvious you care about each other."

The caring was one-sided. "It's not that simple."

"Love doesn't have to be complicated." Raven caught her husband's gaze from across the way and winked. He immediately started making his way through the crowd to get to her.

"You can forget about a happy ending for Cruz and me. He will never be able to see beyond my past mistakes."

His response to Axel's latest attack was proof. Yearning for a different outcome didn't make it reality. She'd accepted that her energies had to be directed to her son's happiness and well-being, not her own.

"You're wrong—"

Raven was cut off by Aiden's arrival. He wrapped his arm around her, tugged her close and dropped a kiss on her hair.

"I have to take pictures," Jade said, unwilling to finish the conversation.

For the remainder of the party, she focused on Henry, which was as it should be. But as they loaded the presents in Cruz's truck, drove to his house and carried them and the leftover cake inside, a storm brewed inside her. An irrational anger suffused her like a bonfire.

While she got Henry washed up and ready for bed, Cruz

went out to the barn to see to Gunsmoke and Old Bob's needs. She read several books to Henry, but her mind was on the man of the house. Henry had fallen asleep by the time she heard the back door open and close, Cruz's boots thud to the floor, one by one, and him lumber through the kitchen to his bedroom.

Without thinking through what she would say, she left Henry's room and strode after him, catching him before he closed his bedroom door. He'd removed his coat and, tossing it onto the bed, returned to the hallway. His tall, broad frame seemed to fill the entire space. She'd never felt intimidated by his size, but right now he was too much for her to handle.

"What's wrong?"

"Why are you doing this?" she demanded, her voice harsh and shaky.

He splayed his hands. "Doing what, exactly?"

"Opening your home. Babysitting us 24-7. Risking your life."

His brows lowered. "You've been in a strange mood all evening. What's really bothering you, Jade?"

"That party was over-the-top." Her eyes filled with hot tears. "Why are you being so nice?"

His lips parted on a breath. "Um…"

"Why act like you care when, deep down inside, I disgust you?"

Anger chased disbelief across his face like thunder after lightning. "Stop."

"Can't handle the truth, can you? Can't handle what I once was?" she lashed out, poking his chest.

"Stop talking, Jade," he growled. His fingers gripped her shoulders.

"You see me as broken and weak and shameful—"

His mouth came down on hers. She gasped. Delight quickly eclipsed her shock.

His lips were firm and smooth, insistent and greedy.

He pressed her against the wall, his chest imprisoning her. She wasn't going anywhere, not when the man her heart cried out for every second of the day was single-handedly tipping her world upside down.

Her fingers curling into his sides, holding him fast, Jade kissed him back with all the fervor he dished out.

Jade Harris was going to be the death of him.

He submerged his fingers into her platinum hair. The strands felt like silk against his skin, as he'd known they would. Her flowery shampoo scent enveloped him, transporting him to an oasis, a safe place where no obstacles existed between them.

She was sweeter than Texas sheet cake and spicier than a ghost pepper.

He cradled her head. Jade was all woman in his arms. So soft. Warm. Loving.

Something clicked into place, and the need to protect Jade at all costs—even from himself—overtook him. He hit the brakes, gentling the kiss until it became a reverent, tentative voyage of discovery.

He didn't want to end it. He had to end it.

Lifting his head, he gazed down into her beautiful eyes that swirled with a new knowledge. A new power.

He cleared his throat. "What you said—"

"Later," she whispered. She brushed her lips against his once. Twice. A third time. Scattering his thoughts.

Cupping her cheek, he softly kissed her temple, her cheekbone and the spot at the corner of her mouth.

She sighed, and he felt that sigh shimmer through him.

It spoke of wistful dreams and star-bright kisses. There was a sad quality to it, too.

Jade knew this didn't change anything between them. He knew it, too, and hated it.

"Mommy?" Henry's voice wafted through the house. "I can't sleep."

"Be right there." Her gaze locked onto his, blazing with longing. She stroked his face with such tenderness that he had to close his eyes against the pain.

She left him there in the hallway.

His phone buzzed. Mason.

"What?"

A pause. "You sound weird."

He disregarded his sergeant's comment. "Do you have news for me?"

"As a matter of fact, I do. The black truck was found ditched on the far side the county."

Their county was huge. "You think Axel's headed out of town?"

"I'm not sure. Did he accomplish what he wanted? Is he the type to change plans when the heat is on? He knows federal, state and local agencies are hunting for him."

Cruz didn't have answers. On the surface, the news that Axel might be leaving the area was positive. Jade wouldn't be in immediate danger. But they couldn't be sure what Axel was doing. Cruz wished he knew, but the only thing he was certain of was that Jade couldn't live under lock and key—couldn't stay here indefinitely.

She had to resume her normal life, and so did he.

NINETEEN

Memories could be both a blessing and a curse. Jade scraped diced carrots, onion and celery into the heated oil and sprinkled in a variety of spices. It didn't help that *the incident* had happened in this house, where she spent half of her time, only steps from the kitchen. She and Cruz were together day and night. How was she supposed to remain logical and impartial? How was she going to purge him from her system?

"Look at my puzzle," Henry called out.

Setting the burner to low, she put the spoon on the counter and crossed to the table. He'd hauled out this puzzle, a gift from Leslie, when they'd returned from another day at the police stables an hour ago.

"Good job, sweetie."

He smiled, feet swinging, as he contemplated his progress. He picked up another piece. "I miss my toys. When can we go home?"

She didn't have an answer to that. No one did.

It had been less than twenty-four hours since *the incident*. She'd yet to let herself dwell on those delightful moments, which meant snatches of the kiss would catch her off guard and send her senses into a tailspin. His strong hands in her hair… Those lighter-than-spun-sugar kisses on her face…

"Mommy?"

She swallowed and, refocusing on her son, caressed his cheek. "I'm not sure, Henry."

He cocked his head to one side, his blond hair slipping into his eyes. "Is this our home now?"

An ache she couldn't explain bloomed inside her. She was content with their rental home next door and had worked hard to put her stamp on it. She and Henry had shared many happy memories there. But this home had one thing theirs didn't—Cruz.

"We're just visiting."

"I like Mr. Cruz." He turned his attention back to the puzzle. For him, the matter was forgotten.

She liked Cruz, too. Liked sharing her days with him.

Popping up from the chair, she returned to the stove. "Are you ready for your performance tonight?"

"I'm going to be the best sheep ever!"

She smiled at his enthusiasm. Cruz had arranged for the unit, in addition to Officers Weiland and Bell, to be at the church tonight so that Henry could take part. Cruz had told her that they'd found the truck and it could mean Axel had decided to lie low or leave the area altogether, and the feds and marshals agreed. She wanted to believe them.

What if they couldn't locate him? She couldn't continue to live here much longer. It wasn't fair to Cruz. Henry was also affected by the unusual situation.

Cruz's bedroom door opened and closed, and he entered the kitchen with damp hair and a neatly trimmed goatee. The smell of his cologne evoked forbidden images.

His dark eyes locked onto her, sending a frisson of longing across her back.

He poked the bag of red lentils. "What's for supper?"

"Lentil stew. I'm in the mood for something hearty and comforting."

"Lentils are not what I'd consider comforting." He picked up the leftover stalk of celery and frowned. "The last time I ate celery, it accompanied a platter of spicy chicken wings."

She burst out laughing, and it startled them both. Their gazes locked across the counter, and she felt a current pass between them. A knowledge that they'd endured trauma together and survived. They'd shared an experience no one else could understand.

How could she find humor when their situation was so dire? Because he was in this fight with her?

She swallowed against the emotions, lowering her gaze to hide her longing. He didn't need to know she would like him to walk around the island, tug her against his broad chest and kiss her senseless again.

"Everyone who's had my stew said it's satisfying. You'll see."

"They were probably just being nice," he mumbled, causing her to chuckle again.

After supper, during which Cruz conceded the stew wasn't terrible, they hustled Henry into the truck and drove to church. Trees in the lot had been wrapped with twinkly lights, and giant wreaths adorned the front doors. People were already parking and making their way inside.

Silver and Raven greeted them, bundled in their police jackets and thick gloves, their cheeks and noses pink and breath fogging in the crisp air. They would remain outside, along with Bell and Weiland. Cruz hurried Jade and Henry through the side entrance, where Tessa was waiting for them.

"Mason's already in the auditorium. He's saving seats

for you." She touched Henry's shoulder and pointed behind her. "Lily's over by the window."

He raced into the kindergarten classroom housing the costumes.

"I'll stay with them until they go on stage," Tessa said, smiling. "Then I'll join you."

Jade could see their choir leader, Candace, and several young moms assisting kids into their costumes.

"Everyone, we have half an hour," Candace called out.

Jade and Cruz made their way to the auditorium. Mason waved them over to the middle section, three rows from the front. The stage had been transformed into a holiday scene, complete with the trees and storefronts the parents had built and decorated.

She turned off her phone ringer and slid the device into her coat pocket, content to listen to Mason and Cruz talk about work.

Cruz sat close beside her, his shoulder and thigh rubbing against her when he moved. He looked dashing in his green-white-and-blue-plaid shirt, crisp jeans and cowboy boots. Like her own personal Christmas present. Her tummy did a dance. If only that were true.

The lights dimmed, and a hush fell over the auditorium as Candace came onto the stage and addressed the crowd. Tessa ducked into the seat between Mason and Jade just as the kids filed onto the stage and launched into their first song. Lily waved at Mason and Tessa. Henry tapped her arm and shook his head.

Cruz chuckled, and Jade was filled with wistful warmth. *Why can't he be the one, Lord? Why can't we be a family?*

If only Cruz didn't have a personal tragedy in his life that made it impossible for him to love her. If only he hadn't been soured on marriage.

Ignoring him was impossible. She was aware of everything…his smell, his breathing patterns, his habit of popping his knuckles and picking at loose threads.

Near the end of the performance, both Mason and Cruz received phone alerts. She felt their moods shift as they read the messages and then exchanged glances.

"What is it?" she whispered.

He shifted to whisper in her ear. "Accident victim in the national park. They need our help extracting him. I'm afraid Henry won't be able to stay for the party. Bell will take you home and guard you until I return, which could be as late as tomorrow or the next day. We never know the timelines on these things." His hand rested on her knee, and her skin flushed hot. "Tell Henry I'm sorry."

"The performance was the important part."

The music swelled and, after a standing ovation, the kids trundled off the stage. Parents, siblings, grandparents and other audience members crowded the aisles.

"Mason and I will wait for you outside the same entrance we came in. We have to relay the change in plans to Bell. Weiland might be able to follow you to my house, as well."

His hand skimmed her neck, once again inducing longing.

He's protecting you because he drew the short straw, not because he wanted to. He's taking one for the team.

He'd kissed her because of emotions gone wild. Her frustration had spilled over and onto him, and he'd reacted without thinking.

The progress to the kindergarten room was slow. By the time she and Tessa reached it, half the kids had been claimed by their parents. Lily ran over to Tessa.

"Was I a good sheep, Mommy?"

Tessa laughed and tweaked her curls. "You certainly were, ladybug."

Jade scanned the room, expecting Henry to be close behind his friend. Kai wasn't there, which meant Elaine had gotten there before her.

"I don't see Henry."

Tessa's smile vanished. "I'll check the restroom."

Candace wasn't here. She'd been caught by parents wanting to praise her hard work. Jade approached one of the assistants. "Have you seen my son? Henry Harris. Blond. Green eyes."

The young woman's forehead furrowed. "He went with his father."

Jade's heart turned to stone. "That's not possible."

"I'm sorry?"

"What did he look like?"

"I—I didn't speak to him. We were in the hallway, walking in a long line, and I looked back and saw him. He waved and nodded, and I assumed—" She paled. "Was that not his dad?"

Cruz wouldn't have picked up Henry without informing her. She quickly described Axel, and the woman nodded.

"He had a hat on, but that sounds right."

She had to remind her lungs to draw in air. "Which way did they go?"

"The far side exit."

Jade bolted from the room, not responding to the woman's apology. She nearly knocked Tessa over.

"Jade, he's not in there—"

She gripped Tessa's arm. "Find Cruz. Axel has my son."

Brushing past her friend, Jade raced along the hall and burst through the exit door and into the cold night. People startled and stared as she darted between them. Rounding the building's rear corner, she yelled her son's name. This area wasn't as well lit, and shadows were thick in the children's play area.

There, close to the tree's edge, she saw a flash of white. Henry had been wearing a white shirt.

"Henry!"

She ran as fast as she could. She didn't see the cement curb and tripped, almost falling face-first onto the pavement. Windmilling her arms, she managed to stay upright.

"Henry!"

Surely if he was out here, he'd respond.

She dashed around the dumpsters and entered the woods. An iron hand seized her arm, and she whirled in a circle.

"Hello, Jenny." In the shadows, she made out Axel's hulking figure. With his other hand, he held tightly to Henry's arm. "Welcome to the family reunion. It's time I introduced myself to my son."

He knew something was wrong the moment he saw Tessa's stricken expression.

"Henry's missing." She jogged across the grass to Cruz with Lily in tow. "Axel has him, and Jade's gone after them."

Mason, Silver and Raven pressed in closer. To keep him from losing it? To keep him upright and breathing?

"Where?" Cruz demanded.

She pointed behind her, indicating the opposite corner of the church. He would've taken off running if Mason hadn't thrown his arm across his chest, stalling him.

"Tess, tell us what you know."

"Jade and I got to the costume room, and Henry wasn't there."

Cruz's gut was a ball of nerves. Sweet, vulnerable Henry at the mercy of a hardened felon? He could only imagine Jade's reaction. Her state of mind.

"Where was Candace?" Mason asked.

"Your sister got waylaid. One of the helpers said she saw a man take Henry's arm and wave in greeting from the other end of the hallway. She assumed he was Henry's father. I—I think she's fairly new to town and the church." Her tormented gaze bounced between her husband and Cruz. "Please, you have to find them."

Still blocking Cruz, Mason barked orders. "Silver— you, Bell and Weiland get these people inside. Raven, go back in there and work on gathering everyone into one location. Don't let anyone else leave."

"Yes, sir."

They hurried to carry out his orders.

"Tess, get Lily inside."

She nodded, her gaze lingering on Cruz. "Be careful."

Cruz shoved Mason out of the way and jogged along the building, leaving the activity behind and heading for the woods. Mason soon caught up.

"Hold on, Cruz. We need a plan."

He kept running. "If I were Axel, I'd stick to the woods," he tossed over his shoulder. "I'm going in there."

"I'll search that section." Mason kept pace beside him, indicating the trees spreading out to their right. His hand shot out and snagged Cruz's shirt, and his eyes were fierce. "We do this by the book, you hear? Sound the alarm if you spot them. Don't go in alone."

Cruz couldn't promise anything right now. Pulling out of reach, he pounded past the slides and swings, praying God would orchestrate Jade and Henry's rescue. He wouldn't let himself consider any other outcome.

TWENTY

"How did you find out?"

"The news did a nice little report on the clinic break-in this morning. Included an interview with one of your patients, and she mentioned your son was about to turn six. I did the math, Jenny."

Enough moonlight filtered through the trees that she was able to see Axel's and Henry's faces, as well as the forest floor they trod upon as they went deeper into the woods.

"I want Mommy," Henry cried, reaching for her.

She lunged for him, but Axel held him away.

"Shut up," he said roughly.

Henry's obvious fright, combined with Axel's callousness, made her eyes sting. She also got angry, a desperate kind of anger that didn't include logic.

"Leave him here," she begged. "You don't want to be saddled with a child."

"And miss out on a chance to get to know my only son?"

"You're a career criminal, Axel! An escaped felon. You can't be a father."

"Don't tell me what I can and can't do," he growled.

Their pace was punishing. When Henry tripped and

hurt his knee, Axel had no patience. "Stop crying," he commanded, which only made the boy cry harder.

She clawed at Axel's shirt. "Let's go without him. Just you and me. L-like old times."

He pushed her away, swung Henry into his arms and kept marching. His ominous silence told her everything she needed to know. He didn't want her around. He would kill her the first chance he got. And then what would happen to Henry?

Axel would soon realize that staying under the radar would be impossible. What then? Would he hurt their son?

The trees opened to a gravel parking lot. Spotting a lone car, she panicked.

Jade tried to wrest Henry from Axel's arms. Frightened, the boy started crying in earnest.

"I won't let you take him!"

She kicked Axel as hard as she could in his left knee-cap, and he howled in pain and rage.

"Mommy!"

When Axel bent to grab his knee, she managed to get Henry free and, with him in her arms, started to run. They didn't get far. Axel's meaty fingers wrapped around her upper arm, squeezing until she cried out. He yanked her to the car and, ripping Henry from her arms, shoved him into the back seat and slammed the door.

When he removed a gun from his rear waistband, all the blood in her body pooled in her feet. She put up her hands.

"No, Axel. Not here." Her gaze slid to the rear window, to where Henry's face was pressed against the glass. "Don't do this."

Please, God, do something.

He advanced on her, the veins bulging in his temple and neck. "*I said,* stop telling me what to do." He called her a few choice names. "I should've wasted you the day I stepped foot in this town."

The sound of movement in the trees had them both spinning around, but she saw no one, heard nothing...until a gun fired. Axel yelped and, clutching his arm, fired into the dark woods.

Cruz emerged from the shadows, his gun held aloft. Mason advanced from a different direction.

"Drop your weapon!"

Axel dashed around the hood and dived for the driver's side door.

Jade threw herself at the car, opening the rear door and scooping up Henry as the engine rumbled to life. She couldn't run very fast with him in her arms, and her muscles were taut, expecting to be shot or run over.

The car sped out of the lot, spraying gravel in every direction. As Mason fired at the vehicle, Cruz ran to her, taking Henry and putting his arm around her. He hustled them back through the dark woods and into the church. Once inside, he ushered them into the first room they came to—the pastor's office—and locked the door.

She threw her arms around him and Henry, knocking him back a step.

Tears leaked from her eyes unchecked, and she couldn't stop shaking.

Cruz rubbed her back. "Let's sit."

On the couch, Henry scrambled onto her lap. "Who was that bad man, Mommy? Is he going to take me away?"

Her body trembling, she framed his face with her hands. "No, baby. I won't let that happen. Cruz, Mason, Silver and Raven will keep us safe."

Her son wouldn't detect the thread of doubt in her voice, but would Cruz? She'd been seconds away from death, she was sure of it. Axel had reached his patience's limit.

Cruz snagged a tissue box from the pastor's desk. She used the tissues to mop up Henry's face first, then her own. Mason arrived and informed them that they had put out a BOLO for Axel's car. The FBI agents and US marshals would join the sheriff's department in the search. Everyone was to stay put until they gave the all clear. Then Mason went in search of Silver and Raven.

Henry announced he needed to use the bathroom, so Jade and Cruz escorted him to the nearest one. The hallways were empty and quiet, because the adults and children were gathered in the auditorium.

While Henry was in the bathroom, Cruz took her hand and threaded his fingers through hers. He didn't say a thing. Didn't have to. His brown eyes throbbed with worry.

They both knew this had been too close. Worse than the clinic.

"No more public places," he stated.

She held tightly to his hand. "Okay."

"How did he know about Henry?"

"He said there was a news report."

Cruz's brows crashed together. Releasing her, he pulled out his phone and brought up a local news channel's website. The video recording began with a reporter standing outside the vet clinic and discussing the break-in. The shattered door was visible, as well as an SPD cruiser. When a recent photograph of Jade and Henry flashed onto the screen, she gasped.

"A vet tech employed here at Serenity Vet Clinic was working when the break-in occurred," the female reporter stated. "Jade Harris sustained injuries and was taken to the hospital. While we don't have details, we've been told she was treated and released."

The video switched to a recorded interview, and Jade recognized one of their patients' owners, Bobbie Polanski.

"Jade is such a kind young woman. It's a shame she was hurt. She has a young son… He's about to turn six. Cute as a button. Anyway, she's wonderful with our rottweiler, and I hope she gets well soon."

Jade's ears buzzed. "Henry's small for his age, and he has my coloring. But when Axel heard he was turning six, he figured it out."

His face had hardened into a marble-like mask, and his eyes smoldered. "This should never have been put out there for the public. I'm of a mind to pay the news station a visit."

"The damage has already been done. What would that accomplish?"

"It would make me feel better."

Her fiery Texan was fiercely protective of her and her son, but he couldn't control the flow of information any more than he could Axel's movements. None of them could anticipate the final outcome…whether or not they'd come out the other side of this alive.

Henry woke up multiple times throughout the night, crying and reaching for her. Her heart broke every time. All she could do was pray and hold him until he drifted off again. She heard Cruz pacing in the living room at times, but he didn't come to their door.

He was in the kitchen ahead of them the next morning.

He gifted Henry with a big smile. "Mornin', cowboy. There's a stack of chocolate chip pancakes with your name on them."

Henry didn't react with his usual good humor. Instead, he pressed into Jade's side, his arms locked around her upper legs. Cruz's brows drew together. She shrugged, uncertain what to expect. Her son had been traumatized, and she couldn't guess how he would process what had happened.

"There's whipped cream, too," she told him, stroking his hair. "I don't know about you, but I'm hungry."

He peeked up at her. "*You're* going to eat pancakes?"

She smiled. "I am. Want to put the whipped cream on mine?"

He nodded. They sat side by side in the chairs facing the kitchen. She served up the pancakes, and Cruz brought Henry a glass of milk.

When Cruz had seated himself across from them, he held out his hands. "Let's pray."

His prayer was brief and to the point. Afterward, he talked about his family and the ranch, trying to draw out Henry. But Henry remained subdued. He did eat one whole pancake, along with several strips of bacon. When he'd returned to the guest room, Cruz put down his fork.

"Our work calendar is clear of public engagements until after the new year. With the abundance of law enforcement in town and considering what happened last night, Mason decided against our neighborhood patrols on horseback. Silver called and invited us over. He thought Henry might need a distraction. There's the indoor pool. The animals. The others are coming, too. What do you think?"

"Henry had a blast the last time we were at Silver's." The officer had once called her to check on one of his macaws, and Henry had accompanied her.

"He'll have fun swimming with Lily. Mason and I can hang out in the pool while you and the girls chitchat. You need a distraction, too."

"You sure you feel up to it? I don't think you got any more sleep than we did."

His face tensed. "I wasn't sure what to do, so I prayed. I don't know if you've noticed, but I've squared things with the Lord. I can't do life without Him any longer."

"I'm happy to hear that." She reached across the table

and covered his hand. "I'm grateful He put you in our lives. I don't know what we would do without you."

"I wish I could be what you both need...for the long haul." His throat convulsed. His gaze on his mug, he ran his finger along the rim.

He was talking about the impossibility of a future together.

His gaze met hers, daring her to argue. "I'm not cut out for family. My past is proof of that."

This wasn't news, but it hurt to hear him say it.

"At some point, you have to forgive yourself, Cruz."

He slipped his hand free. "I'm no good for you or Henry or anyone else. I'm meant to be alone. That's what I've resigned myself to. It's what I want, Jade."

Although she didn't believe him, she didn't challenge him. The stubborn cowboy had made up his mind. Only he could change the way he saw himself.

He carried his plate to the sink. "Can you be ready to leave in an hour?"

"We'll be ready."

Jade was weary in heart and body. This situation was painful for them all.

The change of atmosphere was a good idea. Silver and Lindsey's home was the epitome of Christmas cheer, and the presence of their friends was the perfect distraction. Lily's playfulness melted Henry's reserve, and the children hurried to the dining room to interact with the macaws.

Cruz and the men were clustered around the long kitchen island, evaluating the various appetizers and sneaking bites when they thought the women weren't looking. The women were chopping vegetables and arranging them on a tray.

Raven pointed at her husband. "Aiden, I see you."

Aiden froze, a sausage ball halfway to his mouth. He shrugged and popped it in his mouth. "What do you expect, woman? You're the reason I slept late and missed breakfast."

Raven blushed and acted flustered, and Aiden winked at her.

"Men," Raven muttered. "Watch this." She nudged Jade's shoulder. "Lily? Henry? Are you ready to swim?"

The guys groaned as Lily and Henry dashed over to them, begging them to take them to the pool.

Silver placed several ham rolls into a napkin and stuffed a cookie in his mouth. "Let's go," he said, his mouth full.

The kids thundered down the stairs behind him. Aiden and Mason followed.

Grabbing the backpacks, Cruz sent Jade an inscrutable look. "They forgot their gear."

When he was out of earshot, Raven propped her hands on her hips. "Is he being difficult?"

"I don't want to talk about it."

Her face full of compassion, Raven nodded. "Understood."

"Was it your idea to have us over?" Jade asked Lindsey.

She pinked. "We all know what you're going through. I thought being together would help. Silver agreed."

Jade was touched by their thoughtfulness. They'd all set aside their own plans during the busy holiday season to make her and Henry feel better, and she was incredibly grateful.

Tessa pointed to a corner where stacks of white gift boxes and rolls of sparkly ribbon awaited. "You're delivering your traditional gingerbread cookies today, aren't you?"

"Today or tomorrow."

Jade had heard of their tradition of gifting cookies to

their cabin rental guests right before Christmas. As owners of Hearthside Rentals, they went above and beyond for their customers.

"Have you already baked them?" Raven asked, smoothing her long black hair behind her shoulder.

"Not yet."

"I don't mind helping," Jade said.

"I'm no cook, but I can follow directions." Raven laughed.

"The kids could help decorate," Tessa suggested.

Lindsey looked surprised. "You don't have to do that."

"You didn't have to host this gathering, either," Jade said. "We *want* to."

"We'll make a day of it, then," Lindsey announced. Her smile faded, and she pressed her hand to her stomach. "That breakfast casserole I ate earlier isn't agreeing with me."

Tessa wiped her hands on a towel. "Have you had any more fainting spells? Been more tired than usual lately?"

"No more fainting spells, but I am exhausted. Sometimes, when I sit down to watch television, it feels like someone unplugged me."

Jade and Tessa exchanged a glance.

Lindsey's big brown eyes touched on each of their faces. "What?"

"Lindsey, it is possible you're pregnant?"

Her mouth opened and closed, and color surged and waned in her face.

"Let's sit." Jade steered Lindsey into the living room, close to the crackling fireplace and Christmas tree.

"I've been so busy, I haven't paid attention to the calendar…" She pressed her hands to her cheeks. "A baby never occurred to me. What will Silver say?"

Tessa softly laughed. "I know what he'll *do*. Go into

protective overdrive until the baby is five. He'll be impossible, but you're accustomed to dealing with him."

"You need see your doctor to confirm," Jade added.

Raven popped to her feet. "And wait a few days for her to get an appointment? No way. I'm going to the pharmacy."

Jade caught Tessa's eye and gave her knee a commiserating squeeze. Tessa's smile had a tinge of sadness.

Lindsey looked at Tessa. "Is something wrong?"

Raven sat back down. "Out with it."

Tessa took a deep breath. "Mason and I have been trying to get pregnant for a while. I've had miscarriages, and my doctor doesn't know why."

"Oh, honey," Raven clasped her hand between her own. "I'm so sorry."

Dashing away a tear, Tessa put her arm around Lindsey. "I don't want to focus on me right now. We may have a miniature Lindsey or Silver on the way."

Lindsey still wore a dumbfounded expression. "A baby. With Silver."

Jade was thrilled for her friend. She took to heart the verse that instructed her to rejoice with others. Part of her was sad, though, because a baby with the man she loved was out of the question.

Cruz couldn't see past his mistakes and refused to try for a second chance.

TWENTY-ONE

Silver snapped his fingers in Cruz's face. "Wake up, Castillo."

Standing in the corner of the formal dining room, deep in thought, Cruz dragged his gaze to his friend.

"What's got you distracted?" Silver asked him.

"I have a favor to ask of you."

Silver's violet gaze probed his, one gray brow arched in sardonic question. "Shoot."

There was little risk anyone would overhear them. Everyone was busy decorating cookies.

"It's time to pass this case to someone else. You have the most secure setup of us all, and Henry wouldn't lack for things to do." His chest felt tight, and he tugged at his shirt collar. The thought of telling Jade about the switch made him break out in a cold sweat. He dreaded hurting her. But he wasn't the best option for her. He should've seen that in the beginning. Could've saved them all a heap of heartache.

"That is, if you're still willing."

He braced himself for one of Silver's wisecracks. They'd perfected the art of riling each other simply for the fun of it.

"Of course." Silver stared at him. "I have to ask why, though."

He chose honesty. "I've lost my ability to remain professional."

Silver's lips pursed. "Is this truly what's best for them? Or are you doing it because you care too much?"

Before Cruz could speak, Henry ran over. The boy's small hand slid into his, and his big green eyes—so like his mother's—looked expectant.

"Will you decorate a cookie with me, Cruz?"

He couldn't say no, especially knowing he was about to boot him and his mother out of his life. Plus, he didn't really want to answer Silver's question.

"Show me the way, cowboy."

Grinning, Henry led Cruz to the table, then clambered onto his lap and launched into the instructions. Cruz could feel Jade's gaze on him, but he didn't look up.

Coward.

They decorated too many cookies to count. Lindsey and Raven entered the dining room, and he could tell something was up. Raven was about to burst, and Lindsey's eyes looked brighter than the Christmas tree.

Tessa and Jade exchanged private smiles, while Raven called out, "Fun's over, everyone. Let's clear out." Aiden returned from the kitchen, a towel thrown over his shoulder. "We're leaving this for them to clean up?"

"Yep." Raven linked arms with her husband and turned him toward the door.

Everyone evacuated as if the house was on fire.

As Cruz drove the truck out of the driveway, he asked Jade, "What was that about?"

"Why would you assume I know?"

The dash lights illuminated her features, allowing him to see the hint of a smile.

"Because you're not asking me. Therefore, I think you know something."

She paused. "It's not my news to share."

Judging from her tone, it was good news. He thought through recent weeks and landed on the obvious conclusion. "They're expecting?"

She held up a hand. "That hasn't been confirmed by a doctor."

Watching the road, he absorbed the news. Silver deserved this happiness. He and Lindsey would make wonderful parents.

Cruz's heart felt like a stone inside his chest as he thought of all he and Jade could've shared. He learned from his mistakes, however. He couldn't bear to disappoint Jade.

He glanced at Henry in the rearview, then studied her profile, unable to resist asking the question burning in his gut. "Have you ever thought of giving Henry a sibling?"

Sorrow tightened her features. "Don't ask me that, Cruz."

He was silent the rest of the ride.

When his property came into view, he leaned forward in his seat, and his hands tightened on the wheel.

"Light's on in the barn."

She stiffened. "You don't leave the lights on."

"No, I don't." Parking close to the house, he grabbed his weapon from the glove box. "Stay here."

"Wait—" She put her hand out.

"If I'm not back in five minutes, call Mason."

The cold night air seeped into his bones as he exited and closed his door. The hair on the back of his neck stood to attention. With one final glance inside the truck, he hurried around the house, straining to detect if anything felt off. The silence blanketing his property didn't seem sinister.

Had he forgotten to turn out the light? His schedule hadn't been normal lately, his mind preoccupied.

Gun in hand, he jogged to the barn. His horses came to the stall doors and whinnied. They didn't act out of sorts. He cleared the building. The tack room was as he'd left it. As he emerged, a little boy's cries shattered the illusion of normalcy.

Axel used the butt of his rifle to bust out the driver's side window. He reached in and unlocked the door.

"Get out, Jenny, or the boy is toast."

Her head felt swimmy thanks to the sudden dump of adrenaline. Axel had appeared out of nowhere. The gunshot wound he'd received from Cruz must've been minor, because he wasn't favoring his arm.

In the back seat, Henry was crying and reaching for her.

She turned to him. "I love you, baby."

She scooted across the seat toward Axel, dislodging bits of broken window. He yanked her out and wedged the barrel of the gun into her spine. "Get in the car."

Spying the darkened sedan at the end of the drive, she quivered inside. If she got in that car, she'd never see Cruz or Henry again. She was certain.

Her heart vibrated against her ribs, and her whole body shook with the need to flee. One step. Another. And another. She cast her gaze to the fields across the road. The woods to her right, just beyond her rental house.

The fields were too open. It would have to be the woods.

At the last second, she darted away, dodging his grasping hands. If she could lure him into the woods, there was a chance Cruz could catch up to them.

"You can't outrun me," Axel yelled, huffing close behind her. "This ends tonight."

She veered around trees, got whacked in the face with branches, tripped.

Keep going. Don't stop.

The moonlight glinted off a stream Henry liked to explore. She glanced over her shoulder. Big mistake. Her foot caught on a rock, and she went sprawling. The icy water soaked into her pants and sweater.

Axel's heavy steps registered seconds before a hand clamped on her neck. "Gotcha."

Before she could speak, he thrust her facedown into the water. She choked. Thrashed. Fought to stay conscious.

The pressure eased, and she shot up, gasping and sucking in precious air.

He chortled and thrust her under the water again. This time, the blackness seeped in, robbing her brain of life-giving oxygen. Terror coiled in her middle.

Was this the end?

Would Cruz find her limp, lifeless body in these woods? *God, I'm not ready to say goodbye. Cruz doesn't know I love him. Henry needs me, Lord.*

Axel hauled her out again, twisted her onto her back and loomed over her. Her chest heaved, her desperate gasps breaking the silence.

She tried to scramble back, anything to get away from him.

His massive hand gripped her cheek. His grin was evil in the moonlight. "I'm going to end you, Jenny, and then I'm going to kill your cop boyfriend just for fun. Then I'm going to take our son back to Florida. I think he'll thrive in the family business."

"No!" She gripped his wrist, fingernails digging into his flesh.

He flinched, and she landed a kick to his inner thigh. Jade squirmed out of reach and, somehow getting to her feet, began running again.

His laugh trailed after her. "Still feisty, aren't you, babe?"

Her wet hair slapped against her cheeks, and goose

bumps covered her exposed skin. Her neck and knees throbbed.

Please, God, give me strength. Lead me out of here.

"I like games, Jenny," he called, still coming for her. "And I always win in the end."

TWENTY-TWO

Raven and Aiden careened into the driveway long, excruciating minutes after Cruz witnessed Axel chase Jade into the distant woods. He'd called her and the others from the barn, and Raven had been the closest.

They rushed onto his porch, their faces grim but determined.

"I've got Henry," Aiden stated. "You two, go."

Cruz crouched in front of Henry, who was seated on the couch hugging a stuffed bear to his chest. Tear tracks marred his face.

"I'm going to bring your mom home, Henry. I promise."

Raven shot him a startled look. He'd broken a cardinal rule. This was one promise he planned to keep, however.

Stepping off the porch, Raven paused. "Walk or ride?"

Cruz didn't want to waste another minute, but they'd cover more ground in the woods on horseback.

"Ride."

They hurriedly saddled up Gunsmoke and Old Bob.

"You armed?" he asked.

"Always."

He knew that, but he had to make sure. He couldn't worry about Raven, too. Aiden would skin him alive if anything happened to her.

Cruz's stomach felt like it was in continuous free fall. Dread settled in his bones. He knew exactly how Aiden felt.

Raven put her foot in the stirrup and swung her leg over the saddle. One look at him, and she jutted her chin. "She's scrappy. For one, she didn't get into that car with him."

"I can't..." He swallowed down emotion and ground his teeth. "I made a promise to that little boy in there, and I intend to keep it."

"Let's go get our girl."

The saddles creaked, and the horses' hooves struck the earth in an uneven beat. How much of a head start did Axel have?

Too many minutes for his peace of mind. They slowed often, using a flashlight he'd grabbed from the barn to search for clues. At the stream's edge, he saw Jade's scarf floating half in the water. His eyes burned, imagining what had happened.

They continued to pick their way through the shadowed woods, and he lost track of time. Every minute was torture, because he knew she was facing a monster alone.

The first gunshot startled him. He jerked as if the bullet had slammed into him. A second round blasted through the silence.

"Jade," Cruz whispered.

Kicking Gunsmoke's flank, he urged the horse to go faster than was probably wise. Raven followed close behind.

A third shot raked his ears, and he hunched forward in the saddle. Up ahead, a break in the trees allowed moonlight to filter in, and he saw her.

Jade was on the ground. Looming nearby, Axel shot a fourth time. The bullet scattered the earth near her foot. She screamed and scuttled out of the way.

The brute was toying with her.

Training and protocol went out the window. He called out.

Axel spun and aimed at them. Raven fired her weapon, striking Axel in the shoulder. He stumbled to the side. Lowered his weapon. For a moment, it looked as if he would surrender. Then he glanced at Jade, his murderous intent tattooed on his face. He lunged for her. She screamed and tried to roll out of reach.

Cruz dismounted and raced toward them. Axel grabbed her arm, yanked her onto her back and pointed his gun at her forehead.

"No!" Cruz yelled.

A shot rang out.

Axel thundered to the ground, clutching at his throat and making gurgling noises. Raven had shot him a second time.

Cruz ran to meet Jade. She hurtled into him, sopping wet and shivering. Sobs shook her petite, freezing body.

He anchored her to him, emotion clogging his throat. Over the top of Jade's head, he watched as Raven carefully approached Axel. He had slumped onto the ground, eyes and mouth open.

Jade spoke into his chest. "Is he dead?"

Raven checked for a pulse and grimly nodded.

He rubbed her back. "He's gone."

She went limp. "Henry?"

"With Aiden."

Raven was already on the phone. She waved him on, wordlessly urging him to get Jade home while she waited with the body.

The return ride was accomplished in total silence. In the barn's bright lights, he could see the scrapes and scratches on her skin, her bloodshot eyes, her torn clothing.

"Is it truly over?" she whispered.

He nodded, barely able to speak. His emotions were all over the place and too much to handle.

"You're finally free," he managed, his voice rusty. "You can go anywhere you like. Live anywhere."

She stood with her arms at her sides, her big green eyes locked onto him. Waiting.

He stared back.

She sighed. "I don't know how I'll ever repay you, Cruz." She licked her lips. "Maybe free vet care for life?"

He continued to stare at her, not knowing what to do with the sudden freedom that Axel's death had given them.

"Well, I'm going to pack our things." Her eyes were shiny, and the brave smile she gave him was watery.

She walked past him, and he let her.

Cruz closed his eyes. His life would be empty without Jade and Henry. Joyless. Sad.

But they'd be better off without him.

At the house, Aiden stood off to the side as Jade reunited with her son, his eyes demanding answers from Cruz. *Are you really going to let her walk away?*

He couldn't bring himself to stop her, not even when Henry hurtled into his arms and burrowed his head in Cruz's neck.

Later, Aiden was the one who carried their belongings out the door. Cruz watched from the porch as the trio trudged through the yards. His heart heavy, he returned inside, locked the door and retreated to his bedroom. The police statement could wait until tomorrow. Tonight, he had to come to terms with the dismal future awaiting him.

Sleep didn't come. After a long shower, he thought the post-case crash would catch up to him. He was wrong.

Tossing off the covers, he padded through the house

to the guest bedroom. He turned on the bedside lamp and sank onto the bed, feeling forlorn. Broken.

His heel bumped against something hard. He bent and picked up one of Henry's books. Cruz had read this one to him several times. He leafed through the pages of vibrant pictures of the planets. The text reminded the reader that God had spoken the universe into being, had created the Earth and everything on it.

Cruz sat up straight. God was all-powerful, and His strength was available for any Christian to access.

I've come at this all wrong, Lord. I was worried about hurting her, failing her, and I would do those things if I relied on my own strength. I forgot that Your grace is sufficient. Your power is made perfect in weakness. I'm weak, but You're strong.

He had to tell Jade how he felt.

He was on her back deck at eight o'clock the next morning. She pulled open the door, her expression troubled. She wore an oversize sweatshirt over green leggings and fuzzy socks. Her hair streamed past her shoulders.

"Cruz, what's wrong?"

"I missed you."

Her brows shot up. "You saw me less than twelve hours ago."

"That's a problem, don't you think?"

She bit her lip, then pointed to the basket he cradled in his left arm. "Is that for me?"

"Yes."

"I didn't know Serenity had an Edible Arrangements store."

"We don't," he admitted sheepishly. "I went to the twenty-four-hour store and bought the fruit and these stick things. Uh, this is heavy. Can I come in?"

Scooting back, she waved him inside. He set the basket on the dining table and glanced around. Not much had changed since he'd been here last.

She touched one of the cantaloupe pieces. "You did this all yourself?"

He stuffed his hands in his pockets to keep from touching her and rocked on his heels. "Turns out dipping fruit in chocolate is a little harder than I thought, but it's easier than trying to carve it into something resembling a flower. You should see my kitchen."

She didn't say anything. Just kept staring at the bouquet.

"Um, is Henry sleeping?"

"It took him a while to go to sleep last night."

"I didn't sleep at all."

Jade looked sadder than he'd ever seen her, and he couldn't help himself. He closed the distance between them and lightly gripped her upper arms. "I don't want you to leave." Her brow creased. "I know you can't stay at my house, of course. What I meant was I don't want you to leave me."

Her gaze was cautious. "I can't change my past, Cruz."

"After the clinic attack, I let you believe that your past was a deal breaker. That wasn't the problem. I failed you that night, just like I failed Sal and Denise. I was already falling for you, and I couldn't forgive myself for letting Axel hurt you like that. I've realized that I will fail you. I'm not perfect. I'll make mistakes and act like an idiot sometimes. I'll disappoint you and make you want to pull your hair out. But that doesn't mean we can't be together. With God as our foundation, I'll love you how God wants me to love you. I'll be the husband and father that I'm supposed to be, as long as I let Him guide and strengthen me."

She blinked up at him. "Husband?"

"I want to marry you, Jade, if you'll have me. First, I'd like to go on a real date, and not just to the Black Bear

Café. To a swanky place where you can order the biggest, freshest salad in town, with homemade dressing."

She giggled.

"I also need to see how good you are at mini golf and go-kart racing."

"That's important."

"We'll have to take turns cooking. I can only handle lentils fifty percent of the time."

Jade ran her hands up his chest and around his neck, almost causing him to lose his balance. The look in her eyes made him want to kiss her senseless.

"I can switch things up and serve pinto beans, instead," she teased huskily.

When her fingers delved into his hair, he groaned. "I'll eat beans every day for you, woman."

Cruz lowered his mouth to hers, catching her cinnamon-flavored lips and expressing exactly what he hadn't allowed himself to feel or think or say. She clung to him, kissing him sweetly and intently, as if she couldn't exist without him.

Long minutes later, they resurfaced. She hugged him, pressing her cheek to his galloping heart.

"I love you."

He buried his face in her hair. "I love you, too."

EPILOGUE

"He's going to spoil her, you know." Tessa sank into the lawn chair beside her and pressed the frosty can to her forehead.

Jade smiled. Her husband held their daughter in his arms and was gazing at her with pride and wonder as Mason looked on. Bella Marie Castillo had been born two weeks ago. She'd surprised them early, and they'd had to postpone the baby shower.

"He's so sweet with her," she said. "He's been patient with Henry, who has a tendency to smother his new baby sister."

"Henry's at a good age to help. Lily's jealous. She can't wait to meet her sisters." Tessa rubbed her swollen belly.

"I'm eager to meet them, too." After trying for so long and suffering several miscarriages, the couple was finally growing their family. "I'm glad our children are going to grow up together."

"The mounted police unit looks very different than it did when I first arrived in Serenity," Tessa said.

"God has been generous with His blessings."

Pink and gold balloons strung between the trees danced in the light breeze. At the snack table, Aiden balanced Jaxon—one of the two foster placements in his and Raven's care—on his shoulders while Raven helped Adelaide fill her plate. They were hoping to adopt through the foster care system before adding biological children to their family.

Silver and Lindsey were seated at one of the round tables, a high chair between them. They were trying to cajole their brown-haired cherub, Alec, into eating pureed squash. He wasn't having it.

Lily and Henry chased each other around the yard with water guns, whooping and hollering, enjoying a carefree day. As childhood should be. Jade was grateful Henry wasn't dealing with issues related to Axel's campaign of revenge.

Cruz and Mason ambled over.

"Ready to eat?" Mason asked his wife.

"I could go for cake," Tessa said.

He grinned and turned to Cruz. "She's as bad as Lindsey these days. Always searching through the cabinets for sweets and grumbling, like I hid it or something."

She held up a finger. "Don't play innocent. You did hide the doughnuts."

"After you ate mine and left me nothing for breakfast."

Cruz chuckled and nodded to Jade. "This one swore off smoothies three months into the pregnancy. Can you imagine that?"

Jade shrugged and held out her hands. "Bella must take after her daddy."

Cruz carefully placed their daughter into her arms. He'd been overly cautious with her in those first few days, but his confidence was growing by leaps and bounds. Jade touched a fingertip to her daughter's silken cheek. She had a cap of dark hair and a bow-shaped mouth. This pregnancy and birth had been so different than Henry's. Fear and uncertainty had been replaced with love and support from Cruz, as well as her circle of friends.

When she lifted her gaze, Tessa and Mason were already ambling toward the snack table, and Cruz had filled the vacant seat beside her. His gaze was warm with admiration and boundless love.

They would celebrate their first wedding anniversary next month, and he still had the power to make her knees go weak with a single look. He leaned in and pressed a tender kiss on her lips. Her pulse quickened.

He shifted away with regret. "I have to go to the airport soon and pick up your parents and sister."

Jade was excited to introduce them to Bella. This was their fourth trip to Serenity in the year and a half since Axel's death. She wished Grandma Hazel could make the trip, but she was too feeble. She, Cruz and Henry had made the trip to Florida twice, however, and she'd been able to visit with her. Her family had been shocked to learn she was alive and eager to resume their relationship. They hadn't made her feel ashamed for her poor choices. They adored Henry. They'd also welcomed Cruz into the fold without hesitation.

The Castillos had treated her and Henry with similar openness. When they'd made the trek to Texas, she and Cruz had sat down with his parents and brother and explained everything. There had been many tears and hugs and much love shared during that visit. Hope for the future, as well.

"I'm glad the house next door was available. Between your family and mine, we'd be bursting at the seams."

She and Cruz had gotten married the summer after their fateful Christmas together, and when they moved, her landlord had turned the bungalow into a short-term vacation rental.

He cupped Bella's tiny head. "We'll probably have add on anyway, considering the number of kids we're plan ning to have."

"You indicated you wanted two. Three at the most."

"I've changed my mind." His gaze found hers, and he gave her a heart-melting smile. "I'm thinking five or six."

Jade grinned. "You won't get any arguments from me."

She'd walk with confidence into the future—whatever it might bring—with her husband at her side and the Lord guiding her steps.

* * * * *

If you enjoyed this story,
look for these other books by Karen Kirst:

Targeted for Revenge
Smoky Mountain Ambush
Mountain Murder Investigation

Dear Reader,

Redemption is a beautiful thing, isn't it? I'm grateful God offers each and every one of us redemption through Jesus Christ's free gift of salvation. The Bible tells us that He removes our sins as far as the east is from the west, and I find that very comforting. I like how Jade clings fast to that promise and doesn't let anyone, not even the man she's falling for, lay her already-forgiven sins back at her feet. She's a success story. A new creation in Christ.

I enjoyed Jade and Cruz's journey. The story wasn't easy to write, and I experienced many doubts along the way, but I'm pleased with the final product. I hope you are, too. I also enjoyed showing our other Smoky Mountain Defenders characters and how their relationships have grown and changed. I feel good leaving them with their new and expanding families. Thanks for joining me for this mounted police series set in my home state of Tennessee.

I look forward to hearing from you. Contact me at karenkirst@live.com. I'm active on Facebook, and you can find information about my books and sign up for my newsletter at karenkirst.com.

God bless,
Karen Kirst

SPECIAL EXCERPT FROM

LOVE INSPIRED SUSPENSE
INSPIRATIONAL ROMANCE

Danger comes to her small Alaskan haven.

Read on for a sneak preview of
Hunted in Alaska *by Jill Elizabeth Nelson,*
available December 2022 from Love Inspired Suspense.

The sharp tang of wood stain teased Hayley Brent's nostrils as she dipped her two-inch-wide brush into a can of thick sable-brown liquid. Deftly, she removed excess stain against the lip of the can, then brought the brush to the work in progress. This piece was her magnum opus thus far in her career. The immense and graphically detailed chain saw carving of an eagle clutching a salmon in its talons loomed four feet taller than her five-foot-eight-inch height

As Hayley reached her brush back toward the can of stain, a deep-throated bark shattered her concentration. Frowning, she went to the screen door of the shed where she did her work. A rumbling growl drew her gaze to the right. Her deep-chested Alaskan malamute stood stiff and still in the meadow. The breed-distinctive plume of his tail curved across his broad sable back, hairs bristling. Something wasn't right.

Hayley's gut clenched. "What is it, Mack?"

LISEXP1022

Hayley stepped out the door. Suddenly, a red-and-white aircraft broke into view over the tops of the trees, sparking an explosion of throaty barks from Mack. The unfamiliar plane dwarfed her Cub. Hayley's gaze riveted on the tail of the plane. No identifying numbers or letters. Lack of a call sign often meant one of two things—poachers or smugglers. Dangerous people.

With one hand, she shaded her eyes from the westering sun and stared up into the cockpit. The plane skimmed low enough that she made out the figures of two men. The one seated in the copilot position seemed to get agitated at the sight of her. As the man gestured toward the pilot and then pointed at her, he waved a bulky black item in the air: an automatic assault rifle.

Ice congealed in Hayley's lungs. Nearly everyone in the state of Alaska owned guns, but full automatics weren't the norm. Those were mostly in the hands of the military, law enforcement or crooks. These guys weren't soldiers or cops, and they were not happy to see her.

Don't miss
Hunted in Alaska *by Jill Elizabeth Nelson,*
available December 2022 wherever
Love Inspired Suspense books and ebooks are sold.

LoveInspired.com